THE SHAPE OF HIM

Gill Schierhout was born in Zimbabwe in 1967. She graduated from the University of Cape Town, South Africa in 1994 with a doctorate in Public Health. She has held academic appointments at University College London, the University of Cape Town and the University of Witwatersrand. Twice a finalist for the HSBC/SA Pen literary award, she was shortlisted for the Caine Prize for African writing in 2008.

T0333103

GILL SCHIERHOUT

The Shape of Him

VINTAGE BOOKS
London

Published by Vintage 2010

2 4 6 8 10 9 7 5 3 1

First published in Great Britain in 2009 by
Jonathan Cape

Vintage
Random House, 20 Vauxhall Bridge Road,
London SW1V 2SA

www.vintage-books.co.uk

Addresses for companies within The Random House Group Limited
can be found at: www.randomhouse.co.uk/offices.htm

The Random House Group Limited Reg. No. 954009

A CIP catalogue record for this book
is available from the British Library

ISBN 9780099535775

The Random House Group Limited supports The Forest
Stewardship Council (FSC), the leading international forest
certification organisation. All our titles that are printed on
Greenpeace approved FSC certified paper carry the FSC logo.
Our paper procurement policy can be found at:
www.rbooks.co.uk/environment

Mixed Sources
Product group from well-managed
forests and other controlled sources
www.fsc.org Cert no. TT-COC-2139
© 1996 Forest Stewardship Council

Printed and bound in Great Britain by
CPI Bookmarque, Croydon, CR0 4TD

For my parents

'The figures as I look at them grow smaller and smaller. The more I look, the smaller they become. The spaces between the figures, these vast spaces, have become as important as the figures themselves. My work of six years could fit into a matchbox.'

Alberto Giacometti

1

Herbert Wakeford stops his work and listens. It is as if the air has stilled just for him. The small birds newly settled on the camel-thorn start up their call, then give way to the cicadas' hum. The big, light sky pulses wave after wave of heat and brightness. When Herbert's back stiffens, he starts up with the pick again. He is pulling the rocks away to expose the gravel bedding. In the afternoon, as the shadows cast by the sweet thorn and aloes grow four, five, six feet across the scrub, he comes up to help Niklaas Patience with the washing pan. The two of them shovel the newly sieved gravel into the basin, four feet in diameter. Herbert turns the handle at the side, keeping the stirrer in motion. Niklaas pours the bucket of gravel into the cradle. The larger bouncing pebbles are tossed aside over the top as it rocks. The finer gravel, where the diamonds will be found, falls through to the container on the ground.

Despite the churning of the water, a stone must never float, so the concentrate and sludge go in too, to get the right thickness. The heaviest gravel containing the stones sinks; the lighter spins away, spills over into the centre and drains away. There is seldom a diamond sparkling amongst the pebbles – that would be a find, a large stone like that.

In the evenings, when the stars come full out and the heaps of gravel glint in the moonlight, each one sitting motionless in its own deep pool of darkness, Herbert remembers the reason that we are here. *It is for the sake of the old riverbed, pot clay and calcrete. This is what we collect, and rock and wash and sieve and sort out on the sorting table, sheltered from the sun.*

It was around then, sometime in 1930, that Herbert and I parted ways. It is quite fitting that Herbert should be re-living one ending now, when another is nigh.

We had a neighbour there in Bloemhof – a Chinese woman called Leah Li. One day that year of 1930, Leah was heavy with birth-pains. She laboured to the sound of raindrops lashing the mud plaster off the walls of the diggers' houses, turned to sparkling colours as their pebbles were exposed by the rain. If it had rained any longer the houses themselves might have collapsed. That storm-washed afternoon, Leah Li's first son was born. Leah named him Li Herbert Quan.

When the rain stopped its falling, Leah stood in her doorway looking out. Her skin was red and blotchy with fatigue. The little babe was pressed to her chest. Leah stood watching as every last resident of Bloemhof spilled from the shacks and houses. Their eyes were fixed on the earth, looking for diamonds that may have been uncovered by the storm. They were all dressed in their finery as if it was a Sunday party. For years after, Herbert told all who would listen that his neighbour's babe there in Bloemhof carried a part of his name. Relaying this piece of information always made him glad. And all this whilst his own lady remained barren

2

as the soil in Vryburg's gardens, barren in all the years he knew me.

Yet I am stronger in Herbert's mind today than Leah Li. And he too, God only knows why, lives on strong in mine. If only my bond with Herbert were as simple as a piece of the imagination run amok, if only a few well-chosen chidings would bring my unruly thoughts of him to heel.

Herbert Wakeford sits on the edge of his narrow bed in Doornfontein Hospital. Memories vibrate before him like the mirages seen on hot afternoons in Bloemhof's digging fields. The edge of the iron bedstead is hard and cold against his thighs. He does not recall whether or not he slept last night, despite that it is morning now and the stars are already beginning to fade. Herbert leans over and picks up a small leather-bound book from the table beside his bed. He brings the book closer to his body and then, to better see the cover, he holds it out to the shaft of light that falls in from the passage. How does it come to be in his possession now? Herbert caresses the spine. He once gave this book to me. He once felt my body solid and happy beneath his fingers. How tenderly he had searched out the spaces in between the small bones of my spine, as if checking that each cartilage was in its place.

Herbert grunts, satisfied. Well, a part of him is satisfied. Another part, just as true, must have wanted more.

There are those in Doornfontein who say that Herbert's mind is shot through with holes. He knows what they say, and that they say this because of his condition. Yet Herbert still remembers so much. He recalls how to winch down to prospect a pit and how to cast aside the

3

top to get to the gravel and how to dig a tunnel beneath in a circular drive of a figure of eight so that the pillars remain to support the overlay. He knows that it is better to murder a baby in its cradle than to nurse un-acted desires.

And there is another thing he has not yet forgotten – that 'bandtoms', those banded iron-stones, smooth grey rocks with coloured threads wrapped around, and 'loopers', that look like marble, are the same sort of weight for size as stones, and foretell a good find. Big stones always come in twos and are often found right on the bedrock floor, so clean every crevice in that floor sweeter than a baby's bottom. How he knows these things Herbert cannot say. And this whilst he cannot remember a simple thing – like putting tobacco in his pipe or zipping up his fly. Herbert will sooner forget the life we shared than forget his knowledge of the stones. He has always chosen hard concrete things to love; it has never bothered him that they are not altered by his gaze.

The small beginnings of crickets' chirpings start up outside. Herbert raises his head to greet the square of sky that is visible above his bed. This, his only small window to that quiet exhilaration of the dawn. They only unlock the doors here at 7 a.m. when the nurses change their shift. Still some hours to go now. Yes, Herbert knows quite well how I once lived with him at the diggings. He knows it is where he bought the book that he is holding now. He does not know why he bought the book, only that he bought it in Bloemhof and one evening by the light of the paraffin lamp in our corrugated-iron house, he gave it to me. He took the flint to the fire that night and, because it was a special occasion, lit the lamp. So careful. A thirsty brute it was. Pouring fuel was equivalent to pouring money into its sturdy base and setting it alight. That was the last time Herbert trusted himself to light a lamp. We were sitting on the upturned crates that we used for seats. The lamplight sucked the brightness from the stars themselves and built our bodies' ravines deep with their light and shadow. And only then did Herbert push the book into my hands. His arms shot out longer and with more velocity than he had expected.

'For me?'

Herbert had wanted to make me happy even as he felt himself slipping away. All the simple things he did then, he did them for me, not for himself. He must have known that something was drawing to a close. We sat together until the lamplight itself began shuddering.

It was the nurses in the hospital who told Herbert that I could not have read the book of poems he gave me. The poems were in French. Though Herbert was a man of languages, French was not one of them. And as for me, I speak only my home tongue. I have never had occasion to learn another. And so the nurses in Doornfontein wondered aloud and in Herbert's hearing why it was that I had remained silent regarding his careless choice in the matter of the book. How had he not noticed what he was buying? What use was a book that you could not understand? Had I been trying to shelter Herbert from his mind, a mind already pick-pock marked with holes?

'Stay with us, Herbert,' they said. 'We won't pull the wool over your eyes. In this place we say it how it is.'

Here in the hospital, where they burn the lights all night, where the silence is never pure or fresh, Herbert sits alone and recalls the stars of Bloemhof's digging fields. *They did not have stones there in Mesopotamia where the Bible was written long ago, else they would have warned us to be careful of them in the Good Book. Harder for a camel to enter the eye of a needle than those who love stones to enter God's kingdom. Gold, Frankincense and Myrrh. No, they would have brought the baby Jesus cleavages, stones, makles, yes and milkies too, those cloudy stones that many who don't know think are worthless, and throw away. But once the clouds are cut away, the milky shines the brightest of all, fetches the highest price.*

The stones found in the river gravel are whiter and purer than those taken from the mines. The mine commissioner there in Kimberley knew that too. He made it easy. A digger just had to sign a paper and pay the money to the inspector and it was done. Herbert's favourite finds were from the fields around Bloemhof, then after that Hoopstad, and further up to Barkley West, Verlorenshoop, Moonlight Pool, Delpoortshoop, Gong Gong. Why was it that we worked two claims, not one, all those years ago? Herbert had nailed a sign to a stick and planted it in an empty half-drum, packed about with rocks.

Wakeford and Highbury, 1928

Herbert stepped back to admire his handiwork and he stumbled. He fell onto a cairn of cast-off granite and veldspar, hitting the hard bones of his seat against the rocks. For days after he had a bruise and swelling so dark against the white of his flanks, that tenderest most gentle part of his skin that so seldom saw the sun. Was that the last time Herbert plucked a ripe Tsamma melon growing on its vine out there in the veld, broke it open, squeezed the bitter juices directly on his tongue? Herbert was frail, yes. See how he fell. Just the essence remains.

The patch of sky visible through the window above Herbert's bed grows slowly brighter as the room itself fills up with the light. Herbert examines the cover of the book, the golden brown of it, sun-ripened wheat, the colour of Sara's hair, the colour it used to be. He opens the book. The pattern of the typescript looks so pretty on the page. The way Herbert moves is like none other – he has always been like this. He is Adam himself, taking the very first steps from innocence. He is small and frail and slowly receding. See how he closes the cover as gently as he can and rests the book lightly on the shelf beside his bed. And then again, this reminds me of myself as a young girl, maternal instinct concentrated in a small body, wrapping a doll in a blanket.

Herbert's mind is not empty as he sits here in the hospital. He has not forgotten the special occasion of the day, this, the day that the Lord has made. And if Herbert might have forgotten, he could not, for there before him, draped over the back of the upright wooden chair that has lain empty for the past fifteen years, lies a suit. It is draped carefully so as not to crease. The thin stripe of the suit picks up the early-morning light.

Jane must have warned him not to dress too early.

'Else,' she said, 'your suit will crease.'

And she had smiled her broken smile then and crossed his palm with a finger.

The sticky smell of porridge from the kitchen down the corridor wafts across the courtyard and into Herbert's room. That is one good thing about Doornfontein Hospital – they serve hot porridge every morning for breakfast: oats, white meilie pap or, for a special treat, the malted pap, Maltabella. Judging from the smell, today it will be meilie pap. They always burn the meilie pap.

Doornfontein is more than a day's journey by train to the closest shaft: Bertha, at Balmoral Platinum. Yet even today, Herbert can taste the dust of the dumps on his tongue; even now so far away, he can smell the waste fires that are constantly burning. *The power of the old mines came from human flesh. Bone and muscle, blood fresh and pumping, powering the transition from rock to coal. Sweat and heaving, and the oil starter motors at the shaft station. Four one-tonne coco pans suddenly leaping upwards towards the light. Sorters at the surface picking out the detonators, stones and lower-quality coal like so many pecking pigeons. Looking out for unexploded detonators that would earn an extra thruppence. Holding out palms to the miners on their way up the shaft. For the unused ones, a miner might get an extra cigarette or a bit of pocket money.* And this is how Herbert sits in the semi-gloom and recalls the mines of his childhood. Those were not the diamond mines, but the coal and gold mines across the Reef, and east towards Pilgrim's Rest. That place that stays in your mind, its grasses and stones and dirty streams. His hands and knees were always stained from climbing the trees beside the railway line. Had he climbed up there to hide from something he cannot now remember? I have always

8

understood this about him: it is better to drop into the world like a comet, like a falling star.

When he turned sixteen, Herbert would not go beneath the ground. It was not for him, he said, to be trapped in a labyrinth of stopes that were hardly fit for a rat, let alone a man. He would not be held under three miles of rock, with the only way up being in the cage. For the measure of a man cannot be counted in the tonnes of ore brought to the surface, nor the depth of trenches dug. Of what use are these plain counting things – the like of which the cruelty of playground taunts are made?

Herbert has never regretted his refusal to go underground. He did not mind the money he had to forgo: you earn twice as much underground as on the surface, that is why many do it. Others do it for the thrill of never knowing whether or not they will come out alive, or whether others will carry out their corpses, boots blown off ahead, for the miner's boots are always the first to go. Keep your boots on, and you will live longer! Herbert has never been that physical sort of a person. Instead, he manned the weighbridge. That is where we first met. Herbert did not like to walk on the paths, not then nor anytime in his later life. That is how he recalls it now, walking off the paths. For Herbert knows the power of the earth – its lines and pulls and shifting plates. To him it has always been a kindness to avoid the scars of the well-trodden tracks, to move lightly outside of them, finding his own way through the veld. And those walks! How the sun used to beat across his back and shoulders through the thin once-white cotton of his shirt.

Whatever else Herbert forgets, he will be forever

cursed if he forgets that it was I and not Jane, nor any other woman, who was unafraid to walk with him in the spaces between the vegetation. That one memory surely must always be a part of his make-up, just like the stones. Herbert walks wide-open at the feet now, like a baby. He has not been out to walk alone for several months. On a bad day, the nurses make him sit in a wheelchair to go into town.

Herbert lifts his hands up to the morning light, turns his palms to examine their white calluses, formed from pushing the steel wheels of the chair, and the scar here across his fingers where they caught last time in the spokes. The hard white tissue so unnaturally raised above the rest, but just as true. What kind of a place is this? And why has Herbert not been out walking for so long? They are keeping him captive, a prisoner in Doornfontein Hospital. They wish to keep him here to dig in the garden and empty the slush pails.

'We need you, Herbert,' the nurses tell him. 'There is no one else here as strong as you.'

But if he is strong, why do they wish him to sit in a chair?

There are many things about this life that Herbert does not wish to accept. He puts his head in his hands and he feels its weight. It is not the weight of the skull that is his burden now. It is the soft composition of the musings themselves. For it is here, sitting with his hard head held gently in the cup of his hands, that Herbert sees suddenly and for the first time how his thoughts have been compressed in Doornfontein. Dull-sponge man of him, he sees how pliable he has become,

10

saturated now with the opinions of others, leaving no space for his own judgement. And so Herbert's beautiful head sits heavy in his hands on this particular morning, for are not all things both heavy and beautiful in self-realisation?

When he looks up, Herbert sees his shirt glowing like a harebell in the semi-gloom of the morning, there where it lies, draped with his suit over the chair at the end of his bed. He moves over to reach it, stretches out his arm to take it in his hands. He smooths out the collar and then pushes his right arm into the cave of the shirt, looking about for the hole of the sleeve. He is sitting partially in the shadow of the wall and so he cannot see clearly what he is doing.

The kitchen staff start work early. They leave mid-afternoon and the evening meal sits spoiling in the ovens for the rest of the day. Still, when Herbert smells the porridge and he hears the clatter of the dishes in the kitchen, he knows that the day has begun. By the time the light has grown strong in the room, every button is fastened, including those at the cuffs, and there are no gaping holes. Herbert checks these details and he is satisfied.

It is perfectly light now. He gets up, reaches beneath the mattress and pulls out a small wooden bottle. He shakes it, checking for the sound he knows so well. Then he unscrews the cap and tips a small triangular-shaped diamond into the palm of his hand. Herbert holds the stone out, slightly away from his body, away from his juddering shadow. For a while he gazes at its stillness. Within the sparkling stone, as if etched into its centre, is a triangle, and, deeper in the stone, another within

11

that shape's borders, and a smaller one still deeper within that, and still another, and then, because of the weakness of the human eye, a person cannot tell whether there are any more.

See the crack here through the side? This type of stone is called a cleavage. Maybe a half-carat. But there are stones there the size of rocks, each place with its own common kind of stone. You never refer to them as diamonds. Never. Everyone just calls them stones. This is the kind of thing that Herbert would say, if anyone who cared to listen was nearby.

It may have been Herbert's passion for something outside of himself that drew me to him: but what kept me there long after our time together was over? Why is it that however strong my desire to let him go, there is a deeper desire within that will not broker reason? And more, and more, smaller and smaller like the man he is, receding, and yet still so very near.

* * * *

I see today that the seasons have started to turn. It is almost autumn now. There is a slight chill in the north-western wind. I don't like to think of Herbert there in that cold place that is Doornfontein Hospital. It is a soulless place where the wind blows cold down to your bones.

I sit here in Streuban's Boarding House sheltered behind the curtain, working on the day's crossword in the newspaper. Forgive me that I lose focus on the task at hand. I have done the crossword every day since arriving here in Cape Town, one so easily blurs into the next. I have become the kind of person I pity, the kind

12

that, were it not for the crossword, would most probably not be aware of the day of the week.

My office is separated from the reception desk by two heavy curtains. They are lined with gold and red tassels reaching right to the floor. In the early mornings I organise the menus, send the girls to do the shopping and replenish the cleaning equipment. Then in the quiet part of the afternoon, I sit here in the office. I come here to rest, do the crossword, write a letter, or just sit with my thoughts swirling all about. At least three times in an afternoon the small round silver desk bell that is fixed to the reception counter gives its short sharp ring. I wait an interval to show that I have been busy. Then I come out to the client to give or take the room keys or attend to the complaints.

The first person to ring that service bell was a resident by the name of Floss Streuban. It is odd now to think that that was just a matter of months ago. I feel now that I have known Floss almost all of my life. Floss lives in Room 60, Ground Floor, a special room with its own small garden and positioned at the end of a long corridor. She wears her grey hair long, parted in the centre and braided into two plaits folded and pinned across the top of her head. That first morning, she rang the bell and then, mid-sentence, having barely greeted me, she shuffled off down the corridor to give instructions to the girls in the kitchen about the cooking. Floss is the wife of the owner, and, from the first, Mr Streuban had my sympathies. I see now that he developed a soft spot for me, on account of the kindness I showed to his ailing wife. And yes, whenever his business interests bring him back to town, Mr

Streuban welcomes me into his large office behind the house and asks me how I have been keeping.

Floss usually gives a long ring of the bell, as if resting her elbow on it. Mr Silverstein, on the other hand, always rings in short tones, three strikes in quick succession. Yet on this particular day, early in the morning, it is a different ring – like nothing I have heard before. I wait, listening. Perhaps it is the silence before a sneeze. I wait – but nothing further. One ring, no more. I lean forward in my chair and peer through the crack between the curtains that separates my office from the reception itself.

My heart sets up a strange sort of flapping in my chest.

'Deliveries at the back, sir,' I call.

'I am not here to deliver,' the man replies, impatient, blurring the hard edges of his words together the way an Indian is often wont to do. 'Not to deliver, Sara. I am here to receive.'

Though the beard is gone, and the golden flesh of his face is spongy now, there is no mistaking those hooded eyes, those short arms that hardly seem to come up to the waist of their long mis-matched body.

'Amin Hafferjee,' I cry aloud.

I stand and motion Hafferjee into my office straight away and I pull shut the curtain. I do not want to be seen talking to this Indian Quality Controller from H.D. Jones Fruit Processing. What happened once between us is an historical fact, yes. But I would rather that it remains buried. I see no need to bring it out into the light. Here Hafferjee stands at my desk. I could lose my job because of him.

14

Why have I let Hafferjee in today? I could have turned him away, told him that I was disallowed from receiving visitors during working hours, told him that I was disallowed from receiving an Indian in the house, told him anything, and he would have accepted it and walked his sloping awkward walk, away and on down the street. But it is too late now to turn back. I have already welcomed him in. Is it just that I have always been too open with men, always welcomed them a little more than I should?

I check behind Hafferjee's form as he comes into my office. No one sees the way he enters, stooping, though the doorway is more than sufficiently tall for one such as Hafferjee. I motion him towards the chair. This is not an empty apple crate or an old car seat, such as I used when living in Brakpan. No, this chair is real office equipment and it runs on castors. Through the curtains' crack, I note the disappearing form of Floss Streuban. Her scalp gleams white at the parting of her steel-grey hair. The shuffle of her slippers turns the corner to the dining room. I pull the curtain more firmly closed so that not a slit of ourselves is visible.

'Look at you. All these years have passed and you do not wear a suit! Have you come to place an order for a suit? I don't have my machine here in the Cape.'

Hafferjee pushes past my words, comes right up to me and turns up his face for his lips to greet my cheeks. I tilt my head away. Still his rough shavings disturb the small curled hairs of my chin. Clumsy, there is no mistaking. He does not pursue the matter of his greeting, but settles himself in the chair. Hafferjee, it seems, expects

15

me to be the same as when he had last seen me at Pauline Kraemer's house. That was eight or nine years back now. Does he not understand how much has changed? That day I had flung him from the house with a shrill cry that he should never return.

'You have not changed a bit,' Hafferjee says.

Hafferjee himself has grown very round and his short frame cannot carry indulgence. His skin has darkened over these last eight years, not like honey any more, more like molasses now, thicker and more viscous. His fingers are part-embedded in his white handkerchief, anxiously wiping his forehead and the flanks of his face where the sweat is already gathered into shiny globules. My eyes rest for a moment on those short fingers. Something familiar here. I had not previously noticed how stubby his fingers were, long ago when I knew Hafferjee better than most, when he knew me. I let my eyes rest there a little, watch the white moons of his cuticles rising, and wonder what it is about the human body that makes us see some things about a person at a particular time, while others, just as true, are not seen at all.

I ask after his family.

'They are all well, thank you, the boys long since graduated from college.'

College. I look at Hafferjee with a new respect.

'Have their own families now.'

He mutters something about pictures, bringing pictures to show me. But still he looks out of place here in my office. The old rivers of desire that had once carried our moments together are all dried up now. Ugly riverbeds exposed with all their debris. Later, looking again, the image differs – as if what was seen was simply the picture formed by the patterns of light and shade within a child's kaleidoscope shaken.

'How did you find me?'

My voice surprises me with its hollowness, an abrasive sound that hurts my chest.

'I need help, Sara. Not money. No, not money. Have plenty of money. I will pay you. Tell me how much you charge.'

Back in 5 minutes. Thank you for your patience. I place the notice on the reception desk, propped up against the silver bell, and return to where Hafferjee sits uncomfortable in his smock. I see that he has pushed a small leather satchel beneath the chair. It is aged, pale leather, perhaps springbok or kudu, light in colour and fastened with a brass buckle. Hafferjee will most likely forget this satchel. I must remind him to take it with him when he leaves. I see how his dark eyes are taking in the skin across the back of my hand – it crinkles into tissue paper as I splay my fingers out.

I have a kettle here in my office, and a small tray. I put the kettle on to boil and busy myself getting out the cups.

He says, in a voice that is surprisingly gentle: 'Tell me about your life, Sara, before I burden you with mine.'

The tea here in South Africa is not the same as English tea. It is a different sort of beverage. I've sometimes thought it strange that it has the same name. But to Hafferjee, there is no difference. He takes things as they are. This, I realise now, is one of the things I have always admired in him.

17

I take hold of Hafferjee's hands. They are smooth and warm beneath my touch. I am almost fifty years old now. No one has yet taken sufficient interest in my life to hear its tale. I take his hands and I carefully wrap them around the teacup. I have made his tea black with no sugar as he always liked it. Hafferjee knew me before the young girl Aloma Margaret Proctor came into my life. I was someone before that child made of me a mother. I reach out for that self, that carefree person that Hafferjee once knew – that is what I hold through holding his hand.

I settle back in my chair and I begin to speak. Unaccountably, I am plump with the telling.

It must have been six months ago now that I left Brakpan. There was no one left to watch me go. I boarded up the windows and locked the door behind me.

Vacancy: Manageress for a Boarding House Establishment. Sea Point, Cape Town. Experience required. Temporary Position. Respond in Writing. Excellent References required.

It was a fortunate thing that I had seen that notice in the newspapers. Had I not run my own factory once? Had I not had my own trading store in Pilgrim's Rest? I took a week to write my own references and took care to make them excellent. But not so fine that they would not be believed. A good job, board and lodging. As it was a temporary position, I took nothing with me to Cape Town, not even my sewing machine. I left Frank and Sybil's house just like that. It took nearly three days to reach the Cape, all the way from Brakpan. I am surprised now how easily I left my sewing machine there, for the business of cloth and haberdashery had served me well. Indeed, apart from my current position in the boarding house, it has been my main livelihood all my life. Twenty-five years in this country is a long time, almost a lifetime for some people. Miners, for example.

Frank once told me that the lifespan of a miner is shorter than that of a man in active service. On average, a miner has seven years from the time he goes underground. That is a fact given out by the insurance companies. And most go underground at sixteen. I don't know why Frank was lucky whilst others were not: blasting accidents, mostly, or gases; sometimes falling rocks.

I bring my hands together, wringing them. It sounds so desperate, doesn't it, for a person to wring their hands? I know of people who do that, as a trademark. It is not the way I usually am. I know that it's because I am in mourning here and far from whatever it is that might comfort me. I am not talking about England now, but about the mines up north, the place they call the Rand or Reef. That is the place where I became the person I recognise now as myself. That is my home.

My fingers have always been thin and bony, but recently I've noticed how, at the hard stone of the joints the wrinkles ripple outwards so far as to meet the wrinkles from the next joint, hard stones thrown together into a turgid sea. Floss Streuban is playing the wireless down the corridor. She favours the shows with panellists giving expert views on health and hygiene and matters of child rearing. There are so many crackles across the sound waves that one can barely make out what she is listening to. She walks about with that transistor radio from one room to the next. Floss will soon put the radio in her room and leave to have her hair done. She has a standing appointment every Thursday afternoon at 2 p.m., at the Feathers' Hotel. I can hear the crackle of the wireless but I cannot hear what they are saying. It is of no consequence. Nothing can change what is already done. I tug at the joints of my fingers, those same fingers that reached out to touch a man called Herbert Wakeford all those years ago.

Before I met Herbert, and after, I traded in cloth – I think I have mentioned this already. There were many women in the Union of South Africa who aspired to be sewing, but could not get the bolts readily. I bought from the Cape, and sold up to Pilgrim's Rest in the north-east following the gold rush. Then I travelled to Kimberley in the west after the news of diamonds. I chose and carried the cloth myself, and made good sales. My business grew by word of mouth. I knew nothing of men at that time and was beholden to none. My mother had taught me all I knew about cloth, the importance of examining its warp and weft and how to recognise the strength and weakness of its threads. I cannot picture her now, except with pins sticking from the sides of her mouth like some giant voodoo doll.

But yes, for as long as I can remember, I have loved to walk. And so one day, after meeting with the mine wives' group, and showing them my book of fabric samples, I set out away from the town. I walked along a dust road leaving the civilisation of the mine and the head-gear stark against the sky. I came to a place known as Clewer Siding, near Witbank Colliery. And there I came across the tall pillars of the weighbridge against the sky. All alone up the steep embankment of the line, like a small wound as wide open as a hand against its rocky expanse, I saw a man before me. Herbert Wakeford.

He held the chalk in his left hand to write figures on his slate. Then he took a paint-laden brush, marking the level of the coal on the inside wall of the truck. I could not gauge his age, so at first I hung back a little, watching him for quite some time. Being a woman, I did not want to approach him if he was still a boy. For at first it seemed that his movements were those of a young child, as if he had not known his body all that long, had not had the time to distrust it. But there was something else. His mouth every so often curdled into disappointment and conjecture. These signalled him to be of suitable maturity and so I came forward.

He said that he was Herbert Wakeford, employed by the mine to man the weighbridge. He waved his paint-laden brush between us, splashing the thick whiteness of the paint against the truck as he spoke.

'I mark the level of the coal as it leaves the mine so as to tell the ships at harbour what we sent. There are poor people waiting near every siding between here and the port, with sacks and spades ready to help themselves.'

The clatter of a truck approaching began drowning his voice. I still think of these people he spoke of, people stealing coal, poor and cold, thieves by circumstance or design. It is strange to me now that Herbert's place of origin seemed of such little consequence to me that day. What mattered instead was that he was deep-rooted right there alongside the road. I see now that it has always been like this – Herbert being completely at home on this earth in the place in which he finds himself.

Had I then nodded at the man standing there, thanked him for our conversation, and walked on, none of the events that happened after would have troubled me at all. But once it became entangled with Herbert Wakeford, my life was no longer my own. It obeyed a different set of rules that even now seems to lie just beyond my ken.

I pushed him roughly with my words, afraid of his silence, and afraid at what he thought but did not say. 'Well, what do you do then to these poor thieves? Is there a guard on the train standing watch to arrest them? Are you proud of stopping those poor and desperate from stealing the coal? What happens to these people?'

Still he said nothing.

I was angered by this, and pushed him more with my look and a shrug of my shoulder, as if to signal my departure. Is it not true that a bully is not only the one who shouts, but also the one who is silent when he should by rights be speaking? Thinking of it now, it is strange to me that I did not see his weakness that day. In the years that followed I would have many occasions to bear witness to Herbert's frailty.

At last he said it out loud.

'Nothing. Nothing. Nobody stands guard. Nobody watches the coal. It is just to show at the depot where we filled it. That's all. They estimate the loss, how much in pounds or pence according to the price of coal and how far it's dropped. I write the weight here.' He turned towards the left-most corner of the wooden truck. 'They do the workings at the other side.'

I followed his gesture with my gaze. The line snaked out of sight, cutting through some rocks and trees growing lush in the run-off from the slope. It is remarkable how clearly I can still see that slope and the line disappearing around its bend, if I try hard enough. It makes me think that you could live almost your whole life over again, if you wanted to – which is nonsense, of course. What then is the purpose of memory, this facility that in Herbert was so confused?

I sat on the embankment that day for some time, watching him. His delicate ankles showed beneath loose-fitting trousers that were a little too short for him, as if they had once belonged to someone else. I watched the movements of his long toes feeling around for grit in his open shoes. Out beyond, a wind cock turned in either direction on a distant church steeple, breathing the purity of air. And then a breeze came up and blew away the afternoon heat. Herbert set about fastening down the canvas that began to slap itself against the trucks in the wind. Before he had finished, the rain began to fall. I moved to stand beneath the bridge. He worked without a coat. The skies opened with their flooding and Herbert stood firm, as if he were a rock on a shoreline, the waters draining off him and out to sea.

After his shift was over, we walked together along the Delmas road, and then due south across the veld to reach the Olifants River. From there, Herbert led the way along the watercourse to the confluence with the Ogies, and we came to the Standerton Dam. We pushed our way through the tall grasses to reach the water's edge.

It was there that I watched a water spider hastening away from the reeds, leaving behind a small skid path on the water's surface. Then the spider stopped and began to tussle with a dragon fly, causing its delicate wings to be weighed down by the water. I thought to reach out to somehow save the insect, deter the predator, but Herbert came alongside me, putting his hand on my arm to hold me back. I noted with pleasure the shape of his sandals and the upright way he had of standing. Then I saw that a handful of tiny pebbles and more were hidden in the folds of his clothes. He took them out one at a time, loosely in the flesh of his palm, and with his whole body's motion, sent them skidding, dancing, hopping, climbing across the water's surface, each knowing its own brief moment of glory and then sinking into the water's small motion. It was only later I considered that Herbert had brought us to the eastern shore for a better view of the sun sinking over the water's expanse.

After a time I heard Herbert laughing, a throaty laugh that seemed to issue from the rocks themselves and fill my body's ravine's deep with its awful shadow. It did not matter to us that the grass was still wet from the

24

afternoon shower, we left our bodies' imprint in the grass that day. And then without saying much, we walked back to town in the falling darkness. I was surprised that night to find that I was unperturbed by the thought of Rinkhals or night adders, for I have always been afraid of snakes. With Herbert, my fear was still there but not as a thing to stop me, it became a different thing – fear was something to move through, just like the grasses. And so from that time onwards, I walked through my fears with Herbert alongside, despite his frailty, despite that he was the last person who ever could have saved me.

And so we joined together, Herbert and I. We lived as man and wife. I stayed with him in his rooms in Witbank at first, and then we moved together to Sallies Village in Brakpan. I cried when we moved there, although we gained all the modern conveniences of a proper underground mine, something else was lost. We lived there together for several years, it must have been, in a small mine house just up the road from the compound. Our place was nice and neat with a picket fence to keep in the goats. We had no need of a fireplace in Brakpan for with Herbert, a candle flame could warm a room. I fell asleep like that, with the candle burning, and Herbert blew it out – night after night. Herbert was much in demand then as a compound manager – he spoke all of the native languages better than the natives, or so I thought. Hearing voices outside our house, I could never be sure which was white and which black. Every day the slow trains approached coming from the mine. They stopped there on the weighbridge, wherever we were, their trucks heavy with coal. I feel as if I have spent a lifetime listening to the clank clank clank of the train crossing the line. That has changed now, the joins are further apart.

We often went out walking from Brakpan. 'Let's go up this way,' Herbert would say. His desire followed no human logic. I see now that this is one of the things that I learned from him – how to love desire, to value it above all things. And perhaps one day, following his whim, walking through the broken scrub, we would come upon the burnt-out shell of an abandoned farmhouse. Even now the carcasses of the Boer War still litter this landscape. Yes, this did happen. One day we walked just as Herbert wanted, this way and that, and then over the rise, there stood a ruin. Beside it, a broken windmill clacking. There must have been a hidden current of wind coursing overhead. We walked towards the deserted building, traversing old terraces of gardens and a long-ago orchard. Although the birds had long since taken ownership of the apples, we stopped to pluck a fruit and take a bite. Approaching the farmhouse, I could see that the door was missing – burnt or stolen, or broken up for firewood. The place demanded silence of us, and we gave it. We walked through the house finding nothing of any value. Lingering for a while in one of the rooms, I stretched out my hands to stroke the whitened powdery bones of those who died here. Their spirits lingered all about us, watchful.

I still remember how fitfully I slept that night outside beneath the stars, for I could not sleep in a dead woman's house. Herbert joined me after a time. Inside the house he had woken to the scratch, scratch of a scorpion on the folded jacket he used for a pillow, right beside his ear.

At one time we must have been short of cash, perhaps Herbert was between jobs. More than once we would go out and look for piecework in one of the nearby towns. Once we went to a place, I forget the name of the town – perhaps it was Ogies, or Delmas itself, or even one of the towns further south and west near Kimberley. No matter. We approached the hotel there. The building had a frontage identical to the Queens in Springs, only it was called the Royal Hotel, and very fine. I saw through the door that the carpets were gold. Perhaps here there was some work to do, a little sewing, or Herbert could fix a water pipe or mend the hinge of a wardrobe. A young woman with a child gripping her knees came out to greet us. No work here, things are quiet these days, she said. We were offered water and stayed for a few hours. The boy rode a rusty tricycle around the side veranda, his bare limbs already smudged with its red polish. I remember how Herbert showed the boy some tricks, making patterns with a loop of string stretched between his open hands, in and out with the fingers, like needles. The boy and his mother shared a room here, in return for helping out at the hotel. When we said goodbye to these two, there was a sadness to it, as if we had known them all of our lives. I don't know why that was.

When I think of Herbert now, he seems to me to be more closely related to a stick insect than to a man. He seemed barely human, barely fertile.

*

27

I did not see the small beginnings of Herbert's illness at first, the way his body became disconnected from his soul. And I dared not ask myself why I had fallen for a man like this. Even a snail across a rock leaves a trail; not Herbert Wakeford, there was nothing about his life you could follow. He did not wish to leave his footprints behind on this world. He stood so gently, the wind could blow him over.

I am not a woman who seeks out the pleasures of the flesh in the way that some do. I did not come to Herbert in search of the comforts of the body, yet still this happened. One night Herbert and I were out late. We were partaking of the wine offered by one of Herbert's friends, I forget his name now, no matter. The cheapness of the drink did not matter either. I have often thought of that night because of what happened after we arrived home, back in our little room in Brakpan.

It was as if something alighted on my shoulder that evening, the way beauty does – undeserved – a sort of a grace. I recall Herbert's movements against me that night – as insistent, as clear, as desperate as God's own heartbeat. And then those answering waves in the body, those waves we all know about, which do not recognise the physical structures of the female parts, or the veins or tendons and sinews that you might find in *Gray's Anatomy* – that textbook I would later see in the doctor's consulting room in Doornfontein Hospital – those waves tossed me up to the ceiling and stranded me there. That is what happened that night, and it has never happened before or since. I looked down on my body and that of Herbert's. The face I knew as my own

28

was wet with tears, leaking out into the night. I have never told Herbert this, how looking down at our human flesh entangled, I felt nothing else – not sorrow, or happiness, or pleasure, or shame, none of those things, just something I can only now call love. For that is when I knew for the first and perhaps the last time in my life, that it is just as the Scriptures say, that God is love.

The next morning Herbert and I woke together. There was no soft dawn for us – we had slept too long and too deeply for that. Herbert brought me tea by the bright light of day. Without the glow of the previous night's candle beside our bed, his skin was sallow. Without the sound of the night's wind blowing across the rafters of our house, his voice was thin. A few odd dark hairs sprouted from the soft skin of his inner forearm. How is it, I thought, looking at that, how is it, that a few short hours before, all I was concerned with was that thing we have in common with all beasts, the mingling of the bodies' fluids? Later, Herbert sat beside the window, a branch from a wild olive tree taking its shape beneath his hands. I watched him as he sat motionless but for the switch of his arms and hands in silent service to a piece of wood. I left him sitting there and went out to buy the flour for our bread.

It was not the growing hesitation of Herbert's movements that I noticed at first, though I learned later that this would have been the first sign of his illness. It was not the unsteadiness on his feet that bothered me, nor his anger, unpredictable like the gases underground ready to explode. No, it was the holes in his memory that I first became aware of. Herbert could not hide these, however delicately he squirmed. He would forget to bury the rubbish, tie his shoelaces, do up his fly. It was not laziness. I never knew Herbert as a lazy man. I did not wish to shame him and so we never spoke of these things and the fact that he could not be relied on to keep his word.

There were some small things, however, that were hard to ignore. I recall the matter of the groceries. Things were hard then, not like now, in the boarding house – penguin eggs are plentiful here in the autumn and there is meat on the table almost every day, despite that Floss Streuban fancies that the residents should feast on tripe and onions for breakfast, lunch and tea. I am thinking now of that hot still Friday afternoon when Douglas Pitman sauntered across the main street of town almost swerving into me as I crossed. Douglas Pitman had the same position as Herbert, a compound manager. He was leaving straight from the weekly meeting they had with the bosses to report on the conditions there – living conditions, social conditions, fights, cleanliness. Pitman was on his way home to his missis for the weekend. He was carrying a bag of vegetables and fresh meat, a neat grin on his face. He seemed eager to detain me there in the street. I learned from Pitman that this bag of groceries was a part of the weekly wage. Herbert had not come home with these goods, not once. Douglas could not give the reason. Just said that Herbert had refused to take them. Left them there in the boss's office.

'Ask him,' he advised. 'Ask Herbert. See what he says.'

As I began to move away from him, Pitman took an apple from his bag and tossed it towards me. The fruit hit the side of my chest and fell, rolling away so that I would have to stoop to pick it up. Unprepared, I had not been able to catch it.

'That's the sweetest apple you'll ever taste,' Pitman called.

He licked his lips and gave a sort of misshapen grin. 'Tell Herbert how much you like it.'

His eyes rested on mine until I felt their weight.

When I arrived home clutching Pitman's apple, Herbert was seated on the bare ground outside the house, leaning against the wall. There beside him, forgotten in the Venus ear shell he used for an ashtray, his pipe curled up small departing puffs of smoke. I stood before him. He said nothing. I may as well have been a grasshopper all brown among the brown grasses.

'I just saw Douglas Pitman,' I said. The stringiness in my voice surprised me. 'I wish he was my husband. Carrying a fine bag of groceries home. He said you too were owed it, but refused. Where are those groceries?'

Herbert scarcely looked up, a man gone deaf and blind. It riled me, as if I did not know to expect it.

'So? Where are the groceries due to us then?'

In his own good time, Herbert spoke. 'Sara. How could I take those things, and be indebted then to these people, become dependent on their welfare?'

'It is only a perk, part of the wage. Pitman says it was part of the wage.'

'Part of the wage? Pitman says it's part of the wage. The wage. Wage. Stage, put me on the stage.'

His words rolled out of the spittle of his mouth like pebbles from a high-tide sea. Looking back now I see it was the inconsistency that troubled me – not right away, but over time. For Herbert could swing from sense to banality, wisdom to folly, in a second and back again. And he did not seem to be aware at all of the quality of the thoughts that must have moved his mouth.

The doctors later told me how it was hard for Herbert to hold back the moving of the ocean, the echolalia that came in waves, a part of his illness. What was that to me at that time, when we had so little? What was a woman supposed to do? Conjure up a tea out of the fresh air?

'A perk, Herbert, the vegetables, I just saw Pitman. Where are our vegetables?'

'Vegetables? Perk nothing, Sara. It is bribery, pure as that. I took the wage owed to me, no bribes. No bribes.'

Being paid in kind was the way that position worked on the mines – but Herbert would have none of it, he wanted the cash, and he wanted to choose how to spend it. Herbert was pure, not in the way of one who could always fall back on mother's milk, but in the way of one who truly did not care if he lived or died as long as he could do what he believed, and nothing would ever stop him. Nothing. I knew no one else like him, not before or after. Yet he loved the mines too, Herbert did, he loved the mines despite what he said. 'Where else will you get the means to live? You want 'be a prophet crying in the wilderness? Go then, go and eat your locusts and wild honey.'

And so it was that whilst we lived together at the mine, in a little clean house with picket fences to keep in the goats, Herbert began to take up with the ghosts and seldom contributed to the purchase of food or rent. I took care of myself through my cloth trading. That side of life has never let me down. Herbert began to move in and out, some-times disappeared for weeks. Blown this way and that by his thoughts. After one such disappearance he was away longer than usual. Word got out that he was missing and Douglas Pitman was one of the first to visit. I knew he was coming before the knock shook the door. A dog barked in the distance, a mangy hungry bark. It was well past midnight, the moon sat small against the vast expanse of stars. Douglas Pitman tried to have his way with me that night but I did not oblige.

Some months passed by before I heard news of Herbert. He had been unable to find another position, had visited a number of mines, then moved back to the diggings close to Kimberly, his luck down and he left poorer than before. Someone gave him a cow, and they lived together on bran and molasses. Eventually Herbert had found money to get up to Kitwe in the north, and found himself a job as a riveter. There was a lot of work up there, and the pay was good. The bloke in the empty lot where he was staying had said, 'You need a job? Here, we need a riveter.'

Herbert spent the day learning all there was to know about riveting, and the next day a great misfortune had visited him, or so they told me. As he pushed the wheel-barrow with his equipment – long gloves, heavy tools, bags of rivets – a huge strut of timber had fallen from an overhead crane and crushed his skull. They said that he was head-injured. He was sent to an institution called Doornfontein Hospital. Could Herbert remember what he had had for breakfast? Could he remember whether or not he had made love?

It is true that Herbert worked under scaffolding there in Kitwe and that a timber had fallen on his head. This was a good explanation for his condition, one that soon enough become lodged in my brain and amongst people who knew us. But I recall how even before that, the teacup had clacked against Herbert's front teeth. It was an illness too; yes, it started before the timber with an illness. There have been times in my life when I tried to forget everything I had previously seen of Herbert's frailty, tried to believe, as others did, this story of the timber hurting Herbert's head. But if there is one thing that I have come to believe more and more firmly as the years have passed, it is that forgetting is the same as having holes in your mind, hapless spaces through which every kind of beauty can also fall.

I took the slip of paper, with the hospital address all written down, and the name of the nurse to speak to, given by Herbert's workmate who came to tell me the news, stuffed it into my satchel. I did not rightly know what could be expected of a man whose head was injured. Frank, our neighbour, came over, gave my arm a little squeeze in comfort.

Miners lose limbs all the time. Some years later Frank would tell me the story of how he nearly lost his hand in a mining accident. It should never have happened as it did, he said, for he had worked in that particular stope for two weeks already. If only Herbert had lost a hand. A head was a different story.

The sharp pain that I sometimes felt in my back left me the day that I heard of Herbert's misfortune – I have not had it since. I have become as if spun about in a cocoon, my arms pinned to my sides, yet I feel no pain. I suppose it is a kind of a heartache. It is still like that, you know. The sorrow has never left me. Ever since that first public show of Herbert's illness, my body has changed.

I travelled to Doornfontein to see Herbert's condition for myself. A young doctor was gracious enough to call me into his office. He was a polite sort of a man. I considered each of his questions and provided all the necessary information, as far as I could. Then I told the young doctor that it would be best to keep Herbert there in the hospital as I no longer wished to have the man under my roof. After saying this, I felt a strange sort of lightness, a burden lifted, as it is when something long hidden is exposed.

'Before this "Accident",' the doctor asked, 'did the patient use violence or threats or rough talking?'

'He's vegetarian,' I said, as if that answered it.

Even now, in 1945, being vegetarian is quite uncommon. It was almost unheard of then in the 1920s, except amongst lunatics and oddballs, spiritualists, those kinds of people. The doctor looked at me strangely. But it was surely Herbert, and not I, that occupied this nether world. And I thought then of the night, I can't recall how long ago now, sometime before he had disappeared from Brakpan, when Herbert told me that now and then he lifted things, a few pens from the corner shop, a handful of nails, mostly things of little value.

'Perhaps you could bring home something for the pantry?' I had asked, trying not to show my shock.

And then Herbert had moved towards me suddenly, like a spider or a snake, so quick he took my arm and twisted it behind my back, pushing me against the wall.

I dared not look at him whilst he held me there, I dared not flinch. I waited until I felt the cloud pass over him, and then he let me go.

Perhaps if the doctor knew about these things, perhaps he would help obtain the groceries that were owed us. On the other hand, perhaps he would insist that I return the things that Herbert stole. No, on balance, it is always better, when in doubt, to hold one's tongue. So I looked straight back at him and I said nothing of what I thought. The doctor wrote something on the papers in front of him before looking up at me.

'Sara, it is not good news, but you have a right to know. This patient has been diagnosed with a degenerative disease of the brain. Does he have any other family alive now in this country?'

I sat mute as the day I was born.

'Do you have any children together?'

'No,' I said. 'We thought to try but . . .'

'Herbert should not have children,' the doctor said. 'Symptoms such as we see in this patient, involuntary movements, changes in personality, sometimes violence, irrational behaviour, these develop in adulthood, usually in the thirties or forties. The disease comes from the family, passed down through the generations. There is no treatment and he will get worse, not better. We don't know how rapidly. It may be months, years, we can't say.'

'Herbert does not have those things you are saying, but . . . his speech,' I said. 'Have you noticed Herbert's voice? Sometimes it's loud and raucous, as if he is calling from another world. But that is just how they speak there, and at other times he seems to whisper. Would this disease affect a man's speech?'

'Yes,' the doctor said, and a soft look came into his brown eyes.

'You doctors like to give a thing a name,' I insisted. 'So what if Herbert has this disease that you say? What can you do about it? Is there a treatment?'

'No. There is no treatment. He will deteriorate over time, he will never recover. Just be careful. Don't let him have rough foods. He should eat soft foods, mash them as you would for a baby otherwise he may choke.'

'But aren't you keeping him here?'

'We'll keep him for a while, but don't be surprised if he turns up again at home. I don't think at this stage that we can lock him up against his will.'

So that is when I learned the name of Herbert's illness – Huntington's Chorea. It meant nothing to me. A patch of sunshine burning through the window fell on the doctor's hands casting vertical patterns on them from the window's bars – like some sort of a striped animal he seemed, something in a cage. He tapped the desk with his pen. I walked away then, out of the front door and down the steep slope that led away from the hospital buildings. Vrou se Koppie, that small hill to the west that is shaped like a woman's breast, rose up in front of me, its cone-like form all distorted by the rain and flimsy clouds that blew around it. I wished that I could walk away for ever.

They tamed him there. They parted his hair and combed it over to the side. The line was so straight it showed that he had not parted it himself. The hair was held down by invisible threads of glue, not a strand out of place. The warmth of Herbert's breath, and the sun and the way he had reached like a tree for the light, all that had held together his bundle of limbs, was absent. And I feared what it was that kept him so stork-like in front of me, something mechanical and unpredictable about it. The lightness of Herbert was gone. I went to visit him in the hospital each week. And each visit, the way we spoke together, the way I was with him and the things we did and said, weighed heavily on me. The brain is everything. The brain and the body. I cannot say much of the soul, except that, without the brain, what a strange and useless thing it must be.

With the taming of Herbert in the hospital that first time, I knew an uneasy relief. And his condition had a name. Although he would never again return to live as the man I thought I knew, after a month or so he seemed to speak less of things I did not understand. It felt safer to be near him.

'The diamond diggings at Bloemhof cover a large area where the river once flowed,' Herbert once told me. 'In some areas the gravel is just a few feet below the ground. In other places one must dig down eight to ten feet.'

'Ever been to the diggings?' His voice had been so alive that day it thrilled me. 'Come with me,' he had said.

And so one day I helped Herbert to pack his small burlap bag there at Doornfontein Hospital. I signed the papers, led him out by the elbow. Lord knows that if things were as bad as the doctor had said, we should need a little luck in our lives. I took Herbert to God's digging fields, the ones near Bloemhof, the place that Herbert loved.

Did I think then as I shepherded him out from Doornfontein Hospital that there was still time to let him take one last gulp of the life that he loved before his mind closed down? Did I think that it was my place to make this possible? I suppose I must have. No one forced me. I took Herbert from the hospital and I took him to the digging fields because I wanted to. Even now in the boarding house I do as I please. I take a walk to the Company Gardens on a Wednesday afternoon, for example. It is just that my choices seem smaller now – the menus, which of the staff should do the washing of the sheets and whether or not to walk or catch a train. Perhaps there is more freedom now than I am prepared to admit. Perhaps there is still a chance to find the stones that the old people missed.

The water took most of our earnings, one shilling six pence for a four-gallon drum, and still it tasted of paraffin.

So I said, 'No, let us carry it up from the river.'

But carrying water took more time than Herbert cared to spend. He wished only to search for diamonds.

'Buy the water, Sara. Finding one small stone will buy you all the water you'll need for weeks, and more beside. Find a rock, and we'll build a house here, seventeen bedrooms, each with its own bathroom.'

'What are we to do with seventeen bedrooms, Herbert?'

'I'll marry you, Sara; carry you over a threshold of marble tiles.'

Herbert had been in Africa too long; he thought he may one day want more than one wife. Many a woman fancied him then, in an idle sort of a way, not realising how difficult it was to be yoked to a man like Herbert.

We lived there, Herbert and I, and we did almost all of the work ourselves. Only now and again did we have a native to help us on the claim. Here in the boarding house, I do so little myself – there is even a girl who takes care of my washing. One of the residents here, Mr Silverstein, is off to the lavatory again. Prostate trouble, I would bet on it. Going past my office, he treads as lightly as he can. Respect for the recently bereaved, I suppose.

So much of what happened at Bloemhof has escaped my memory now. Piecing the story together in my mind, it seems to me that Herbert and I could not have lasted more than two years together at the diggings. It felt much longer. And yet it is the day we left, the day I was compelled to take Herbert back to Doornfontein Hospital, that I recall most clearly. Strange how the happenings of a single day have blotted out almost everything else.

Later, the nurses scolded me, told me that I should never have taken Herbert to Bloemhof. They said that it was the diggings themselves, the way that everyone we knew had the diamond fever, swore and killed and lusted after the stones, slept on the riverbank to be there at first light, that this disorder fed the wild black things that lay within Herbert, made him lose his marbles sooner than he otherwise might have. But tell me, what do those nurses know of love?

Herbert was out before sunrise. He returned to our little corrugated house at about 7 a.m. I prepared coffee and griddle cakes and porridge for his breakfast. Our little house was silent but for the dry clank of the spoon against his plate and the wet masticating of food in his mouth. Afterwards he washed his cup, plate and spoon one by one. He went to put on his coat. I still do not know why he needed a coat in the heat of Bloemhof's digging fields. I made him promise to come back home when he tired.

It came to 11 a.m. and the sieve still lay untouched at the washing pan. I heard our helper, Niklaas Patience, muttering outside. He had been standing out in the hot sun waiting for Herbert all the morning on the claim. I gave Niklaas the leftover griddle cakes with some tea. He looked at me as if I had asked him to do something against his judgement, and then he left without eating, shaking his head and click-clicking with his plump pink tongue. I have not seen him since. Strikes me now how in the months that I knew him, Niklaas never once looked me in the eye.

That day I too did not work the claim but stayed indoors cutting and soaking lemons for preserve. The shadows cast by the sweet thorn and aloes grew four, five, six feet across the scrub. Just before sunset, I saw the small stick figure of Herbert in the distance. He was dark against the western sky, a man staggering. I filled the kettle, lit the stove. Then all at once Herbert was home, standing at the kitchen door, half-leaning against the doorpost. He could still divine, he said, as his father used to, the dowsing rod shaking side to side of its own accord in the cemetery gardens. His eyes were bright like the stones. He sat motionless and I reached under the sink for the old tin mugs I had but seldom used. Perhaps there is no harm in it, I thought.

41

Perhaps this simple act will help us go back to a time everything was pure. I was thinking then of the day not so many weeks before that Herbert and I had found two decaying bodies, hard and cold as stones, buried beneath the fallen earth, the tunnel collapsed above them. A pair of corpses in Bloemhof's digging fields. The shock of it, and the sky wavering all about me. Herbert had said nothing, yet made the sweetest tea I ever tasted, hot and strong in an old yellow tin mug that burnt against my lips. And although I never had sugar in my tea, the day we found the bodies and searched their orifices for stones Herbert ladled the sugar into that old chipped mug still smelling of paint. Drinking from it, I was not the same woman who had seen those bodies and smelt their flesh. The one who drank entered a different self, the Sara that lived before that horrible event.

I kept back three of the stones we found on those corpses as a kind of insurance. I sewed the first into the top of my black stockings where its weight would rub against my leg. The second, I sewed into Herbert's cap, and cautioned him never to lose it. There I fancy that it weighted his head, and helped prevent the cap from being lifted by the warm autumn winds. I pushed the third stone deep into the hem of my bedroom curtain. That was already my favourite storage place: a lover's note, the key to my safe.

I made the tea for Herbert as he had for me that day. He laughed, and pronounced that I was right about the tea, and I knew he meant about the cups, the old tin mugs in place of china. And so we warmed our bony hands together on our mugs, those marvellous mugs so full of heat you could barely touch them. The cups here in the boarding house are not nearly as comforting, perhaps for being unfamiliar.

Against the dirty yellow of those tin mugs, Herbert's eyes lost their blueness. I knew that it would not be long now, that despite everything we had shared he was entering another realm, a place I could not go. I would not have thought then that it was possible for me ever to forget the colour of Herbert's eyes.

How defenceless Herbert has always been, despite his strength, how terribly endangered.

'Here,' I heard myself say, with a tenderness that surprised me. 'This tea will make you feel better. And then in the morning we need to go to Doornfontein.'

'Please take me home, the bell is ringing,' he said.

And so he curled up on our bed that last time, the shape of the bones of his spine showing up cleanly beneath his shirt. I went again to the kitchen, turned over the timer, and slowly watched the sand trickle from top to bottom through its narrow waist.

The next day after breakfast I made Herbert lie down and rest on the bed whilst I prepared something to eat for the journey, just pap and Herbert's favourite *sous*, made with tree tomatoes, onions, a little garlic added. No meat. I willed Herbert to be vegetarian still, yet if I told myself the truth, I knew from the acid smell on the skin of his neck, and the stiffness of the neck itself when he embraced me, that he was not.

'How long have I known you?' Herbert asked me between the clank clank clank of the train passing the joins in the line on our way to Doornfontein.

'Don't you blame me,' I said. 'You must have been headed for this place before I knew you.'

Herbert tilted his head back and laughed, a deep dark laugh from the newly opened cave at the back of his throat. Despite what I had said about him being headed for this already, I could not help but wonder whether it was being with me that had made him sick. For I have always believed this: in the wet dark places, the body's cells are shared.

I left Herbert and his compatriots there at the hospital. They silently watched my departure through the window's glass. As if I were the weather, some snow falling on the trees, of that much relevance to themselves.

Floss Streuban came by my office yesterday. Floss, who always needs six pins to keep her braids fastened to her head, found yesterday morning that she only had two and one braid left dangling.

'The cleaning girls have stolen my pins,' she cried in alarm, tears filling her eyes.

I reached down into my desk drawer and pulled out a few from the secret stock I keep for occasions such as these.

'Here. I caught the thief red-handed, forced her to return the pins.'

Floss has just left for her hairdressing appointment now. Odd that she spends her money on a hairdresser, for her hair always looks just the same when she returns, re-plaited, pinned.

I tell Hafferjee all of this. I tell him that the man I once loved, perhaps still love, one Herbert Wakeford, had a disease of the mind, the sort of disease that is passed down through the generations. I have never spoken to another soul about Herbert's true condition, never told anyone what a certain young doctor had said.

'Have you heard of such a disease, Hafferjee? You are an educated sort of man, your boys have been to college. Have you heard of this disease?'

And because Hafferjee had been a friend and because our bodies had made themselves molten together beneath the Singer sewing machines in my workroom so long ago, I tell him everything I know. And because of all that has happened, and because of what has brought Hafferjee here to my office in the boarding house today, he hears me, every word.

Conversation heats the blood like honey, Herbert once told me, so that it can flow more easily. I suppose that if the blood stops flowing, a person is no longer alive.

2

It is early morning in Doornfontein Hospital as Herbert looks at the sparkle in his palm. He notes the smooth sharp edges of the stone against his roughened skin. He sees that what must be done this day is what must be done. And he sees no cause for weeping. He considers all of these things and then he tips the diamond back into his small wooden bottle and he replaces the lid.

Many years have passed since Herbert first showed me this particular stone. He thinks now of that day so long ago. A chill wind had come up and we had moved our seats closer to the fire's warmth. He thinks of how after showing it to me he had put the small wooden bottle back into his shirt pocket and begun halving slippery onions in the palm that had so recently held a stone. He slips this same bottle now into the front pocket of his best ironed shirt.

'Ever been to the diggings?' he had asked me.

'Not yet, I plan to go.'

'You must come with me,' he had said.

Why had I not wished to marry him all those years ago? He turns this question over and over in his mind. Marriage is what he would have wanted. Surely he would have suggested it? He does not have the facts of the matter to hand. He shakes his head, sifting a plethora of impossible explanations through the holes in his mind. An early-morning wind brings coldness down the hospital corridor. There is no fire's warmth here in Doornfontein, for it is against the hospital practice.

Herbert has kept this lucky stone close to his heart for how long now? Twenty years? Twenty-five? Almost a lifetime for some people. He has kept it, just for the sake of keeping it. Today is the day he is to be a generous man, and give this stone away. Yesterday he was convinced that this was the right thing to do.

Herbert squirms. The wooden bottle lies small and dark against the white fabric of his shirt. The rest of his clothes are still laid out across the back of the chair – socks, suit trousers, jacket and a tie, each one in its place. But it is the black felt hat, lightly stained with a cobweb, sitting on top of all of the rest, that makes Herbert think of a puppet. The shirt is not there, of course, Herbert has already put that on. Without the shirt, everything looks dark. Darkness. Herbert has never been afraid of the dark. He has had no choice all his life but to embrace the shadows.

When he first settled in here at Doornfontein, Herbert used to go out walking. He liked to set out before the dawn, so that he could be home in time for breakfast. That was when he was still entrusted with a key. Those days are long passed now. He is no longer deserving of trust. They say, as nurses do, that this is for his own good.

Herbert had walked for miles those long-ago days.

Although there were no mine dumps for miles around, he always managed to find his way back home. On one of these walks, he discovered a sulphur spring.

But it is true! Or at least some of this is true. He travelled north-west for a change. The wind took him, walking across the gleaming porcelain plate of the earth. Vertigo, eyelids sticky with glaze, the brim of his hat the upturned horizon, his head light and dizzy with desire. A toppling, wobbly man with sand in his base, rocking around but never knocked over. And then he saw it, felt it, tasted it, this reward from hillsides diseased with aloes and broken rocks. He shook the drops from his hands, brought them to his cheeks. The water left its stain on him. The hot smell of sulphur touched his lips. A sulphur spring bubbles up between sand and rocks down in a vale between a sudden denser patch of scrub and bushes.

How Herbert would have loved to have spoken to me then. He would have said something like this: 'Hot, hot water, it goes on and on. Right at source. Healing, crystals, I know you will approve. Your constitution would be much improved by the minerals. Come and bathe with me there tomorrow.'

The nurses had been quick to tell Herbert that I was far away; a sensible businesswoman by then, dealing in cloth and haberdashery. I was far away in the Cape, far away from Herbert and his mind shot through with holes.

Herbert was alone then, and alone he conceived a dream to open a health spa. He would furnish a room with an old-fashioned chamber horse: all the benefits of a good trotting horse except the fresh air. He'd ride a wild horse himself. It was for the sake of the rich folks, he would get them to pay. And in any case, a chamber horse was cheaper in the upkeep: no hay. And when the place was deserted in the summer heat it would wait, uncomplaining. He raised his idea with the nurses, put forward a case to apply to the municipality for approval that year in 1932. Yet all along it was not the nurses or the municipality that Herbert wished to convince – it was I, Sara Highbury. He knows that now, he remembers it. Herbert's mind was turned towards me like a sun-loving plant to the sun. He did not wish for any other lady to turn her eyes to the cast side of his river, there where the fertile fields lie. He wished for no one but I to come and see what fruit a careful work may yield.

And so one day, despite the distance between us, he left the nurses and the municipality, and he came all the way to my little rented house in the Cape to find me, to tell me about the sulphur spring. Herbert knows that he set off from Doornfontein Hospital, and that he did not walk – it was too far. He must have gone by train. He does not recall where he found the fare. He thinks of that day so clearly now. It is as if he is there all over again – sitting upright at my kitchen table, careful not to spill his tea. He turns the events of the day over and over in his mind, searching for something he only dimly feels is lost, something not quite true. He has holes in his memory, this he has come to accept. But the mind is larger than memory. So much of his mind is still intact.

Anna Papenas could not have been more than twenty years old at that time, yet it was as if the river had already run through her face, left its stain on the land-scape. She stood in my kitchen and looked at Herbert. She had a way of looking at you, that girl. She stood, expecting his response. He was not paying attention. He was trying to stop himself fiddling with his hands or touching things or shouting out. He had asked her for a glass of water, yes.

The sweet fresh liquid gurgled in his mouth. Liquid was a friend to him for it helped to dampen the ticking sound characteristic of his illness. This sound became insistent, louder and louder if he let his mouth get too dry. He rose to open a window. And all the while Herbert's soul was twitching too, like some creature newly hatching from an egg. Or is it only in the present, he thinks, looking back from the safe vantage point that is Doornfontein Hospital, that it seems as if the soul trembled too, along with his body? Was he aware of it at the time, or is this a belated gift brought to him by his mind so torn and broken? In any case, the soul, being largely invisible, has never been Herbert's major concern. It was the body he must control. This young lady would think he was some kind of a madman if he could not keep the body still.

And then, with Anna still standing in front of Herbert at the kitchen table, I was there, standing on the threshold of my own kitchen, looking in. When he noticed me, Herbert stopped his trembling and stepped forward to embrace me. I drew back as surely as if he had reached out to strike me with the flat of his hand. He remembers how I recoiled from him that day. It is a fresh blow delivered now by his mind.

*

50

'How did you get the money to come?'

It did not escape Herbert how I shifted my foot more firmly over the loose floorboard beneath which I kept my purse.

'As a matter of fact, I found myself some work,' Herbert said. This business about a job just slipped out, for my sake. He wanted to be a man again to me, a man who could work. Because this small untruth did not matter we continued the pretence. No, I say it did not matter, but it mattered a great deal. His dignity mattered to me, it always has. Herbert sees this clearly now, as he recalls this day, he sees that I loved him and he looks up again at the small window in his room and he smiles his soft shy smile. He still has all his teeth.

'What have you been working at then, Herbert?'

'As a matter of fact, I, well, I, I found work in a barbershop. Simple work.'

Just that he said it made it feel true, as if it really happened, just like the sulphur spring. And the next day after breakfast, Herbert and Anna Papenas had walked out together into the garden. For a week or two, Anna was Herbert's friend. She laughed to hear he worked as a barber and she let him cut her hair. That hair of hers, long and straight as the roads through the Karoo. They sat afterwards in the cool shade of the guava tree.

After just an hour or two out in the garden, Herbert's thoughts clouded over. His body frazzled as if a bolt had gone through it, draining with it the charge that ordinarily makes up a life. He stood deflated, half-expecting some pain to be inflicted.

'Mind you take it easy now, Herbert,' I called to him from the open door. 'Come indoors this minute and lie down.'

Later Herbert told me about the sulphur spring.

'Just a smelly little hole in the ground bubbling foul odours,' I said. 'Just a smelly wet muddy hole. Even the flies would not go near it.'

I laughed then. Herbert is not troubled by the memory of my laughter, how I laughed and laughed until the tears spilled from the wide-open holes in my face. Then I left him and went out to the late-morning service at church to pray for his soul.

'Still have your soul,' I muttered. 'Pity the brain is so in question.'

That afternoon I took Herbert by the hand to the small outside room filled with old paint tins. He helped to clean it out. This was where he must have slept. He would not have taken liberties in my bed. That day sticks in Herbert's brain like honey. That day contains all the sweetness of the world.

Herbert glances across at the book of poems that he has put to rest here alongside him on the shelf in his room in Doornfontein. Someone once told him that a book is like a garden carried in the pocket.

Is it too early to be putting on his trousers? No, who is to say? He feels ready. Herbert places his hands carefully on the bed, either side of his thighs. He pushes himself up with his fists and walks over to his clothes on the chair. The Karoo sun is already beating through the corrugated-iron roof above him. He hears the crack crack of the roof lifting up on its timbers in protest at the weight of the heat. It will settle down in time when all the iron is heated through. Herbert stretches out his hand to stroke the fabric of his suit. So gently, as if there is no wildness lurking beneath. As if he would never have the strength to follow through with his plan.

The gentle drumming of the Cape winter rain sounds on my roof outside, reminding me where I am. This is how I live my life, now that I know Herbert is gone. I sit behind the curtain and when required, I attend to the residents and their complaints. I do this as graciously as can be expected. None can fault me, for I fulfil each of my duties just as they are expected of me. But it is, as the Scriptures say, as if through a glass darkly. I can find no good reason to laugh.

I have a burlap bag of Herbert's possessions here beneath my desk. This bag that was left to me. I had been disbelieving: what could Herbert possibly have left to bequeath? What is left that the storms of his laziness and misfortune have not washed away? A few old canvas shoes soled with old cycle tyres? And there is a book of poems that once was mine. Looking across at Amin Hafferjee, I am minded to ask him if he can tell me the meaning of these poems, for after all he is an educated sort of a person, and the poems are in French. No, I will not ask him. Something in me knows now that whatever it is that Herbert intended to convey through giving that gift, it is not to be found in the words themselves. I push the palms of my hands flat against the desk.

The location of the boarding house is, as the crow flies, perhaps a half-mile from the house where I came to live after leaving the diamond diggings. Hafferjee knows that house well, for that is where he and I first became properly acquainted. Cape Town has changed, of course. Hafferjee, having lived here through the changes, does not notice them as much as I do. New factories have sprung up, leaking their smoke out into the dark night skies. The chimneys' emissions are not amongst Hafferjee's particular sorrows for, unlike me, he never knew the fresh open skies of Bloemhof's digging fields.

*　*　*　*

After leaving Herbert in the hospital I had gone back to the diggings to uproot the sign that Herbert had planted the year we staked our claim, *Wakeford & Highbury, Two claims, 1928*. Two years at the diggings and I would live every day of it all over again if I could.

I kicked over that sign from its half-gallon drum all packed about with rocks. I pulled out the stick and the signboard and threw them both into the veld that lay beyond the town. I wouldn't have left that sign for others to paint their names in place of ours.

I was fortunate to have kept back a few stones for myself, just in case things with Herbert should turn foul – I suppose that I must have always known that they would. I stayed in Bloemhof just long enough to be rid of the stones. And with the proceeds I bought several sewing machines. I positioned myself in Cape Town to take advantage of contracts to be had there for the finishing and pressing of industrial clothing. Before long I was flooded with piecework and had not a day off. Not like now. Nowadays I have every

Wednesday to myself. I have no washing, ironing or cleaning, for the cleaning girls do it all. In the afternoon I take a walk all the way to the Company Gardens. I like to sit there on a bench in the sun, feed the squirrels, watch the shadow pass over the mountain, and then come home. This is what we have to look forward to, getting older – there is more leisure time, more time to brood.

On this last Wednesday, yes, only yesterday – so much has happened – I walked a different route to the Gardens for I was afraid that Floss Streuban might be following. Not that it mattered, but having heard what I had, I just wanted to be alone. I walked down Castle Street and into the station and right through it, out the other side. This was the place where I had first met Maggie, her upturned face watching the tick-tock of that station clock. The old white clock face is still there, mounted on the wall above the platform. It is now cut across with broken glass. I went to sit on my favourite bench in the shade of the oak trees and bought a cup of tea from a girl selling there. She poured hot water from a large urn into a paper cup. The first taste I had of it burnt my mouth inside with its hot curdled sweetness. From over the cup's white rim, I watched a group of vagabonds seated on a bench diagonally across from me. They were thin and tanned almost black. I couldn't help but think that one of them was watching me. I have been thinking about those men all week, wondering who they were. If only I could tell from such debris as lies at the bottom of my teacup what fate lies ahead for myself. But that would do no good at all. Does a person gain strength from early knowing?

Or is there simply more time to become paralysed by fear? I swallowed the last of the tea, already cold, and returned the emptied cup to the girl. I could have bought a whole tin of tea for what I paid for this one nasty cup.

On the way back to the boarding house, I picked up Herbert's possessions from the police, for Herbert named me his next of kin.

'Is it usual practice for the resident of a mental institution to be allowed a will?' I asked.

The policeman gave me the burlap bag.

'What will you do now?' he asked. As if I had ever depended on Herbert for my welfare, as if I ever could have.

At the time Amin Hafferjee and I met, I was operating my sewing business from a house in Observatory, not far from here. The house was owned by a lady by the name of Pauline Kraemer. Perhaps it is owned by her still. That was fifteen years back but I am past the stage of being awed by years, they pass so quickly. If you opened the front door you would go down a small passage with a bedroom to either side. Those were the workrooms where I kept my sewing machines. Then on to the sitting room that I used as my own room, nice and bright with a fireplace. And after that there was a further small passage that I used for storage. The passage led to the back door of the house and off of it to the right was a bedroom, and to the left, the kitchen. In the back garden, there was a small room with a cement floor. During the winter, the rain blew gust after gust against the glass of the sash windows, each gust bringing a further draught of cold air into the work-rooms. The house was well positioned, not far from the station. In addition to taking in orders, I sold a little fabric and haberdashery. Each Saturday, I tried to interest passers-by in a sale bin of fabric set out at the gate.

I met Cora Rynhardt before meeting Hafferjee. Yes, I have, as she is wont to remind me, known her for longer. She came that first week, a long-legged bird-like woman coming to eye out my rolls of fabric. I have never under-stood what all her scrabbling was in aid of, for Cora Rynhardt does not sew. She is a slight bony woman, with a nervous flutter about her, here in the gesture of her hands, here in her eyelids, a twitch of the ankle. Her walk is uptight and teetering, like a pine about to fall in the wind. Since Cora took such an interest in the sale bin, and was about so often, I tried to interest her in the selling. I have to give it to her – she had a talent there.

And in the evenings we played cards. Cora shuffled the deck so that the cards would fly within the circle of her fingers. It was between hands of Gin Rummy, Snap, Poker, Twenty-One that we agreed that Cora should become a sort of a deputy in the business, move into the spare back room of the house and help with the orders. Cora was the daughter of a chemist and, being unmarried, was still living with her father when I met her. She was happy to escape his pills and stay with me. I owe the success of my business in those early days to her. Floss Streuban reminds me of Cora, here in the scratch of her neck, there in the tilt of her head.

*

Before long, Cora and I had attracted sufficient contracts to employ assistants. We took on young girls as learners. As soon as they knew too much, I would be rid of them and take in fresh blood. Rather that than be forced to pay a higher wage. I do not know what those girls did when they left me. Some would have gone back to the farms, I suppose. Others could take on positions in garment factories, furniture manufacturers, or as tailoresses, milliners, fish canners, upholsterers. There were more jobs about then for a young woman than when I was starting out. They learned from me, I paid them what I had to, and they left. I did not run a charity.

I have heard it said that if you have others working for you, you should not show favouritism, for it creates bad blood. Yet I could not pretend it was otherwise. There were the others, and there was Anna Papenas. Anna was quiet and lent a sort of dignity to the work. Without saying much, she kept the others docile. Lanky wisps of black hair that were as straight as the railway through the Karoo fell across her pale face. She slept on the floor by night, beside the machines. She feared that if some morning she was late because of a tram strike, or some other unforeseen, I would give the job to another. And so she stayed with me through many a contract. Every evening Anna went to classes at night school, Salt River, swaying along Lower Main Road on her black bicycle. Sundays, all the girls had off. Anna studied, and sometimes did further piecework for extra cash. I began to think that she might become a more permanent employee and perhaps in time be trained up to take over a part of the business.

For some time there were the three of us in the house – Cora Rynhardt, Anna Papenas and myself. It was like that when I met first met Mr Amin Hafferjee, his skin like honey then, as I have said already I think, not like molasses as it is now. Hafferjee was a man with all his marbles in their place. A sensible sort of soul. He held down a good job in the factory, worked a regular day and harboured no fancies with stones. His skin has grown darker now. But it is not just his darker skin, his rounder form – there is a sadness about him that I have noted before in men of this age: sad, and slightly despairing. You see this thing called ageing happening to other people, but you do not think that it will happen to you and to your contemporaries but it has.

It is a solace now to think of that first meeting with Hafferjee for I knew such happiness then, a relief from the sorrows that Herbert had brought. Yet our meeting could as easily not have happened. I had printed and left notices advertising my business at Atlas Trading, illegally, just beside the counter where the Indians pay. And Hafferjee happened to pick up one of the notices and telephoned me. So it was that I responded to his request to supply a quotation for overalls. I journeyed to the factory where he worked as a quality controller and I was entrusted with that first order from H.D. Jones Fruit Processing. That was how it happened.

The factory had recently opened and the girls were already complaining that their clothes were being ruined by the acid juices spitting up from the cauldrons. Most of the operations were located in Paarl, a small inland town on the way out to the interior. I journeyed there alone. As it was the packing season, the train's carriages were full of the chatter and banter of wives and daughters come in from the farms. At the factory, the fruit of high quality was individually wrapped in a thin purple tissue-paper and put in crates to send to England. Rotten fruit was boiled with sugars and put in jars.

The girls that Amin Hafferjee oversaw cut and packed pears and apples for canning and preserves. They stood in rows, ten to a bench. Their blades seemed to be extensions of their hands, so naturally they moved. Their straight strokes sliced the fruit in two. The pear halves dropped into their steel-banked rivers, jumped like small rabbits down the conveyor belt, to fall, at the climax, into an enormous cauldron. The more forthright of Hafferjee's girls had come to him, a gaggle of them one teatime. They had elected a spokesman who lodged the complaint on all their behalves, demanded the protection of overalls.

I went up to where the girls were standing alongside the conveyor, for I wished to take measurements. Hafferjee's girls seemed so firmly planted in ankle-deep water, most with wellington boots, others with wrinkled feet, so well stuck that I felt I had to ask Amin Hafferjee for help in uprooting a typical girl, to measure her. A girl, who seemed of average dimensions, came then, and I wrote down the inches of the bust, waist, hips and length. This was the size of the normal overall, and I would make a few larger and a few smaller.

Most of these girls were of the Cape Malay or coloured race. They spoke Kitchen Dutch and were small in form, unlike the African native women, who, although their physical form may be better suited to heavy work, were disallowed from working there. Given the African's differing physical dimensions, my standard ways of measuring would be, in any case, unlikely to produce a garment that would fit. For many such women the widest part is lower than the hip. A different technique is required.

I measured in a curtained-off cubicle on the factory floor. Amin Hafferjee stood to the left of me, looking in my direction now and again from beneath his hooded eyes, watching and stirring and muttering his spells. And when I came closer, he left no room for ambiguity. As if it was a thing a person did every day, Hafferjee reached out to close his honey-smooth hands over my own. His hands embraced mine so gently, and then they were gone. And later, before I left, he touched my elbow. He was a short man, shorter even than I, and so the thick belt of his waist, not his leg, brushed against my hip in passing. That is how I knew Hafferjee – right from the start he made his intentions clear.

Before I left, he slipped me a card, not printed, but written in his own small spiky hand, blue ink. On it, his home address, his family address where he said he stayed most weekends. It was not four or five blocks away from me in the adjoining neighbourhood.

I let a few days pass and then one morning, when the light made out the shapes of things enough to walk by, I dressed and left the house in order to reply to Hafferjee's invitation. When I departed, Anna and Cora were still sleeping peacefully there in the stale shut-up house. Hafferjee did not live far, but I went the long way around, via the mountainside. I marvel still at how Amin Hafferjee, in the ordinary course of a working day, had closed, then immediately released, his honey-smooth hands over the thinning skin of my elbow. He knew a body's skin, knew just what touch could best be felt, as if he knew that day I would be least expecting it.

I caught my breath as I reached the upper contour path and looked out over the vineyards and vegetable fields of Wynberg, across the pine plantations of Tokai, towards the Muizenberg horizon. The Indian Ocean's expanse was still grey, slowly growing a pale pink as the sun appeared from behind its back. In a little while, a wide bright strip of light would cut through the ocean towards me. I recall this walk across the contour of the mountain because even as I put one foot in front of the other, I was still deciding whether or not to go to him. I stepped carefully down from the mountain towards the Hafferjee neighbourhood, a little clutch of houses close to town.

As I came closer I noted that the house was freshly painted. Smudges of bright pink flowers sat in a pot beside the door. I have never been fond of those Impatiens not a flower that can sway in the breezes nor with any sort of a striking upright appearance. Just lies there on the ground, a torn piece of colour, spilled ink across the brown earth, a few pathetic leaves strewn about.

I checked the address against the card he had written. Number 41. I slid my note addressed to Mr I.A. Hafferjee, carefully sealed in its envelope, through the waist-high flap on his front door. As I walked away, I did not turn like Lot's wife to look back, like Lot's wife who was turned into a pillar of salt. Her flesh became granules of salt, standing there, half turned back, for all time, or at least until the rain collapsed her. Nothing in me cared to look back. I did not care what my note to Mr Hafferjee left in its wake.

Sunday evening came around. Just before seven o'clock I put out a piece of tinsel. It was Christmas after all, the season to be merry. I did not bother with mistletoe and trees and suchlike. Just had time to drape the tinsel there over the mantel, when Hafferjee stood at my front door, holding not flowers, but his own fez, snatching it in an irritated fashion from the gusts of wind that shook the street every summer. I wonder now with Hafferjee sitting here before me if he remembers this first time as clearly as I do. We have never spoken of it. We have never spoken of how I motioned Hafferjee into the hall and locked the front door behind him, though it was not yet eight in the evening. The wind caught the door from my grasp and slammed it shut. I had not yet lit the lamps as the evening was not yet fully come, the south-easter's gale still obscuring its quietness.

As he came into my workroom, Hafferjee balanced his fez expertly on his head. Then, as a nervous after-thought, he pulled it off again. I tried to look in his direction. The bristles of his short black hair disappeared into the gathering darkness. He trapped me with his eyes that night; bright they were, a hungry entitled look. I had not been with a man since Herbert had come one day from Doornfontein. That visit of his was the last time a man had stood at my front door. Herbert had moved to take me in his arms in my own house. After, he had walked away back to his home and family in the madhouse at Doornfontein Hospital. But not before he had tried to take me in my own house, and, even though his eyes that day had been as hard and shiny as marbles, for memories' sake and because I had wished not to injure him further, that day I had not resisted.

There in Pauline Kraemer's house in the Cape, with this man called Amin Hafferjee, I heard myself laugh out loud, seeing the word Singer come into focus on the closest machine. I felt like a song in this room filled with machines, with this oddly awkward short-limbed, long-bodied, black-bearded, honey-skinned Indian quality controller from H.D. Jones Fruit Processing. My world flashed through his dark eyes, the black rounded bodies of the machines oozed their gold script, their distorted pedals surprisingly hard against the flesh of my arm, as if something was melting, but the solid not yet fully gone. Hafferjee's short limbs seemed to be everywhere at once, here, then there, and here again, filling every angle of my vision.

As I let him out I felt a splash of fondness for his shoulders that sloped so steeply like a hillside at which I wished to graze again and again. Hafferjee was back each Sunday after that first time, the next week, and the next week after that. And every visit, at 10 p.m. on the nose, his rounded back retreated down the street,

64

to his wife and children. Almost all grown up now, he had said.

Muizenberg beach in the early morning: I took off my stockings. My toes overflowed with cake crumbs of sand. I waded out a little way into the ocean with Hafferjee alongside me. Laughing. It surprised me how the white stems of my legs were at home in the surf.

That Hafferjee was married did not trouble me. Had he not told me (as married men do) that he and his wife had long since ceased conjugal relations? And in any case, I knew that I did not wish to live with a man again, not after Herbert. Those years with Herbert my body bled like a drain for two years without stopping and afterwards the doctors pronounced me infertile. Only much later I wondered if the body mirrored what I witnessed of Herbert's illness: a leeching out of constancy. After all of this, Hafferjee was an unexpected charm, an unbroken shell on a trampled beach.

Was it then, in the sand, that I noticed that Hafferjee's feet were small, smaller than even mine?

I don't believe that Hafferjee and Herbert ever met. That was not deliberate, it is just the way that it was. From the time Herbert and I parted ways in 1930, until they stopped letting him out in about 1933, he would release himself from the hospital and come to visit me in Cape Town. He turned up at least once a year, like the dustbin boys, come expectant for their Christmas box. It seemed that no one from the hospital missed Herbert, for no one bothered to come to fetch him and take him back.

On one such occasion, Cora and I were completing

an order from H.D. Jones Fruit Processing in Paarl. I think, yes I am certain now, that this was the order for the hats. Forty wide-brimmed hats for the seasonal pickers.

How we struggled with those hats. The brim had to be wide, but not floppy so that it would obscure the pickers' vision. The interfacing had to be thick enough to avoid the brim collapsing down, but washable too. It should not lose its shape, had to have a good standard of colour fastness. And when the order was at last ready for delivery, there I was, detained at home with Herbert. I suppose I could have left him alone whilst I went to make the delivery but I did not like to. What if he tried to follow me? Anna Papenas had offered to stay with him.

'Thank you, my girl. But you go to Paarl. It wouldn't be right to leave a young girl with a man who has lost his marbles.'

That is how Anna Papenas made her own journey to Paarl. I did not know at the time that that visit was the beginning of Anna leaving.

I recall she wore her best grey pinafore when she took the trip to H.D. Jones Fruit Processing. White starched shirt with the ruffles to the neck, stockings and boots. I pressed some money into her hand, a packet with her lunch, kissed both her cheeks, and she was off. She carried the hats in a bag slung across her chest. The same journey I had taken some two years before. The factory was situated a beautiful way inland so that the girl must have been breathless when she arrived. I do not know whether or not she had ever before seen the silhouette of the mountains against the sky. Perhaps there was a small party under way when Anna arrived at the factory. Or perhaps it was just lunch break. A confusion of faces, looking and gesticulating, would have directed Anna to Hafferjee's office. His office was set a little back across a newly slopped concrete floor. It was still within the ambit of the cauldrons, their noise and their heat and their sickly sweet smell.

'*Gaan binne*,' the laughing toothless girl who had escorted Anna would have giggled and scampered away.

Did Anna stand for a moment on the threshold and then step inside? Did Hafferjee have his back to her at first? Perhaps he stood up and smiled at the girl standing there. He must surely have closed the door behind her.

I wish now that that doctor had never showed me the picture of Herbert's brain – the brain eaten by this disease. For the doctor held the picture up to the light and he said that as the years passed, the progression of Herbert's illness would be like rats at the fruit bowl night after night – a bite here, a bite there. The purest and juiciest parts of his brain would be the first to go. Seeing the picture of that half-eaten brain, I began to think that Herbert was capable of almost any kind of a misdeed. It is too easy to say now that I should have known to trust my own impressions of Herbert, not the prediction of some doctor who barely knew him.

In the weeks that followed Anna's visit to Paarl, she became more pale and fragile – like the injured bird I had come across one day beneath the washing line. I had brought the bird indoors, put it on some cotton in a shoebox, but it seemed as if my very touch was too much for it to bear, and the next morning I found it dead. Herbert went back to Doornfontein, muttering about Anna – he was all fretful and troubled but being the way he was, I did not listen. And then Anna left – one morning without proper notice, taking her few belongings with her.

The strange thing was that along with her own possessions, Anna took something of mine when she left. I soon forgot about it, but I remember it now, talking to Hafferjee. It was a card Herbert had once given me – a message writ inside:

For Sara.
The full moon floats in your blood.
You give birth to tomorrow.

And at the bottom, it was signed with Herbert's own distinctive, frightened kind of a signature: *Herbert Wakeford*.

White ink on black paper, white on dark, not dark on light, so that the writing looked as if the light had fallen on it. The years' passing, and perhaps the moisture here at the Cape, had rendered the whiteness of the ink grey and ghostlike. I have never understood what it was about this card that made Anna take it. She could have told me. She must have slipped the card into her apron pocket that day before she left.

I see now that Anna Papenas saw what even I did not – that Herbert and I were tightly connected, linked by the light and shade we had lived under. She must have seen then that I would do almost anything for him, anything that would ease his passage across this earth. In taking that card of mine she showed me that she knew this, she wanted some of that connection for herself.

Herbert, like many others in Doornfontein Hospital, became someone who could not remember a simple thing. Like putting on his shoes – he had once walked out to the shops with the others, in their long crocodile, impenetrable in his socks. Herbert had always been unpredictable, this was a part of his charm. Then once in the mental institution that was Doornfontein Hospital, he seemed to find more of himself, was more free, and I, who had wished to anchor him, was more frustrated than before. It was as if he had planned it all.

* * * *

Casting my mind back now to Herbert's visits to us in the Cape, it is difficult to tell one apart from the other. For the one thing, Herbert always seemed to arrive when I was not at home. And so although he only came but once or twice a year, it felt more often for being unpredictable. I would go out on an errand with the lingering anxiety that I might return to find his acrid smell hanging about the passage or his old coat draped on the nail on the back of the door. He always found some new way to surprise me.

I am thinking of this time. I put the key into the bright light of the keyhole, pushed the door into the shaft of light. I was a little blinded at first and so I stumbled over the strip of wood at the door's entrance. The blue and white bread bin had been left open to let in the flies, a plate unwashed lay on a counter. The loose floor-board in the hallway unsettled as I walked across it. I peered into the gloomy workroom. Someone had left her machine uncovered, all open to the dust. I stepped in to throw the cover over. The floor was still strewn about with scraps and threads. The loud grinding buzz of some cicada beetle started up, slow and close it sounded, as if coming from my very own shoe, or just around the corner somewhere, fading in and out as I walked.

I must have brought the insect in with me, I thought. Or there is more than one in here, lying in wait, starting up in welcome as I come within its radius.

'Perhaps those here have gone out, visiting or to the bar for a drink.' I said it out loud. 'I think I will go to wash and then to bed.'

I pushed open the bathroom door. There Herbert lay. His body was flat like a plank, sprigs of dark hair growing out just visible from the pale chest. Not quite flat, of course, oddly interrupted by a gentle fleshy hillock of muscle, and a tiny pink rosebud nipple rising out of the water on either side. He was almost all covered over, with the water gone a dirty brown and a thick ring of scum formed already around the bath. God knows how long he had already been in there. I swear he must have seen me but he slipped his head back under the water. Eyes clenched shut, his head full of suds, a half-smile stuck down there all about.

His head still beneath the water, he lifted up a bony ankle from the suds to scratch at something on his calf. I cleared my throat and gave a little cough in greeting. He shifted in surprise, and reached out his hand to cover the half-erect private parts that lolled about the water's surface.

I will never forget the song he started up, there in the bath, still audible through two closed doors.

'Riches I want not, nor man's empty praise, be thou my inheritance, now and always . . .'

His voice sounded hard as stones thrown against the tin bath. Herbert's voice issuing from his hollow head, the brain itself injured for ever. Stationary for the moment in the bath. I knew from the sound of the voice, and the way that the water splashed in the tub, that Herbert was not improving, no he was not. Not content with finishing his song, he started it up again.

'Nought be all else to me, Save what thou art . . .'

This man singing in the bath was someone out of the ordinary experience of things. The Herbert I first knew would never have indulged himself like this, with singing and splashing; this Herbert was indeed free of himself. There have been occasions I was a little envious of Herbert's oblivion and his innocence. For even that day in the bath he did not care overly much what he did or who he was. He seemed to hear nothing of the relentless cicadas' songs, or the weighty silence in their wake. That beetle, I concluded, must have been in one of Herbert's shoes, the sound coming straight out of its cavity, unashamed, hiding there. I moved towards the shoes to throw them out of the door. Stopped myself just in time, lest I offended him.

Cora watched as I walked across to the kitchen window to close its lacy curtains.

'We all need our rest, Cora,' I said. 'And a man with an injured brain, I am sure he needs more rest than

71

anyone. Who knows where he has been? Sleeping rough, perhaps. We must be careful lest we are forced to take him back to Doornfontein.'

'He is changed, Cora,' I said. 'He smells different. Let him use all our water for his bath, and he will still have this smell. I don't like it, not one bit.'

Even now I can recall Herbert's smell as I had known it in Bloemhof, and when we were together on the mines: that wild mint, and sweet cannabis burnished against the scales of his skin, the warmth of it coming in from the sun.

On the last visit, Herbert came for a reason. I sensed that something weighed on him. He put off telling me. He could not or would not speak directly, and to this day I do not know if it was because he had forgotten what he came to say, only remembering later, or if he was just being difficult, like a stubborn child refusing to put on her shoes. Was it on that visit, or on another, that Herbert came out of the bathroom, stooped a little, freshly scrubbed with Sunlight Soap, a small hand towel wrapped around his waist? Christ himself in a loincloth, he thought he had become, speaking in signs and parables.

'Hold my arm,' I said. 'Here.'

We walked together to the outside room where he always slept. I made up his bed with cushions and blankets. I thought how he must have lovers there in Doornfontein Hospital, and I pictured them with wild eyes, broken teeth. It was my impulse to think of women like this and I wonder now why I did not trust it.

'Mind you take it easy now, Herbert. You go to sleep and I will too.'

Later, I peered through the door to check on him. He lay fast asleep like a child, his mouth flung open to the side as if to swallow the moonlight still pouring in through the window. The oak outside swept the floor all about with its slow shadows of twigs and leaves.

And then two days into Herbert's visit I could take no more and I told him he must say what he came to say, then leave. He said nothing and my insistence that he go seemed to wash right over him as waves over a rock. Turned seamlessly from expecting to enter, to expecting to be turned back from whence he came. I could see even then that this was not a natural way for a man to be. Something in me expected and, because of that expectation, hoped for some sort of a natural resistance from him. But none came.

We walked to the train station. He looked straight ahead and spoke easily of this and that to do with the weather and the people passing by on the street. A band of African children threw marbles at a tin can, their bony ankles grimy with the dust, light mud-stains against their dark shins. I was surprised at the fresh sting that came from the sight of these children – their idle playing reminded me that my time for having a child of my own was over; so quick, it had scarcely begun. An older group, ties loosened from school, leaned watchful against a wall; an old woman began to pick up apples from the gutter, trying to push them back into a broken bag. Herbert wished to stop to help her. I resolved to speak to those nurses, tell them to lock him up, for he was becoming a public nuisance.

I would speak to them, yes I would. It was then that Herbert remembered why he had come to see me. It was then, on the way to the train station, that he told me that he had a girlfriend. Would not reveal her name, came over all shy it seemed.

'There is nothing to be shy of, Herbert,' I told him.

This is what love was like, one just could not foretell it. And if you could, you should not: anything else, but not love. It will be tainted and spoiled, as the white flesh of a lily gathers those brown-veined streaks from too much handling.

Herbert looked for recognition or approval.

I said that I didn't know her.

'But I came here with something to tell you,' he insisted.

And only as the train rounded the last bend before picking up speed on the straight run to Doornfontein, after the sheep field, the glade of poplars marking the last farmstead on the line, Herbert told me that his girl-friend was expecting a child, that they were not allowed to keep it, and perhaps I could think of . . . no, perhaps not, what did I think?

I remained unmoved, for at that moment either I did not believe him or I did not care any more.

'I think you need to go and get some rest.'

'Yes,' he said. 'Rest. But another thing, Sara. Ask Frank, Frank and Sybil.'

'Who? Frank! The bloke who was our neighbour then in Brakpan? What! Do you want this babe plugged up with bran and molasses?'

For it had been from Frank and Sybil that we learned how a cup or two of bran mixed with molasses can be fried into a cake, the cheapest way to fill a hungry belly.

'Frank is bound to have a couple of kids of his own before long,' Herbert said. 'One more won't make any difference.'

My fingers reached out to trace the timeworn parchment of Herbert's neck. Surprised by the wart still there where it had always been. The skin on the back of Herbert's neck had always been as falling scales, soft scales of brown and pink and white where the clouds' shadows had formed a pattern of light and shade, surely these must still be imprinted by the clouds under which he had lived? And yet his skin, as I felt it there, and as I looked again to check this was indeed Herbert, was suddenly smooth and pale, just a flat white, not as I remembered it at all. Herbert smiled then and his smile twisted into a shape that was unfamiliar to me. I pulled back. I could see then that there was more that Herbert wished to say. He did not have to tell me what followed, no, he wished to tell me and I could not stop him. For is it not in the nature of sinners – that confessions are forthcoming not for your sake, but for their own?

Herbert blurted it out: 'Sara, you know the girl. It is your friend Anna Papenas. I met her at your house.'

Strangely, Hebert began to laugh then. That is the sound I remember now, more than any words he said. So physical, it could have come out of the ground itself, both deeper and more ethereal than any sound yet heard.

Was this revelation some new symptom of Herbert's

illness, the confused ramblings of a man dimly aware of his frailty? Why, surely Anna was more sensible than to look twice at a man like Herbert – she had her life ahead of her.

'Anna says that I am the baby's father.' Herbert had the nerve to remain calm – not a tremble or a stutter shook him.

I thought of what I knew of Anna and her family. Poor, yes. Religious, yes. And a younger brother. Anna told me once that the family's hopes were vested there. For them, the present and the future were already earmarked for this boy's education, his clothes, his needs. All this for a boy who had done nothing at all to deserve these things, taking precedence over another child, this child of Herbert's. I was so angry I could scarce remain standing. Recalling this now, I find I am thinking of my own brother. We were children together, at the edges of childhood. I at its beginning, he at its ending. It was a source of shame to me then, not to be a boy. And so I stuffed my long hair into a cap. And how the future of the family rested on his shoulders, eclipsing my own. Yes, there was a time I looked up to my brother and his friends, before I knew better that they were not to be trusted. Even now so many years on I cannot erase from my memory the shifty sad look he had, his half-open breathy smell, his jagged finger-nails and cold hands. I see that this is one of those sorrows that linked me to Herbert – having no family that I can speak of without shame makes me, too, fly into the world like a comet, like a falling star. And so like him, I have learned to find my solace in the way the trees grow in the face of the wind, in the path of a lizard across a rock – the same order of small things that Herbert loved.

'Goodbye,' I said to Herbert that day at the station. I stood on the platform watching as he weaved about through the carriages looking for an empty seat.

Speaking of changing and staying the same, I chanced to look in the mirror this morning. I have been elbowed aside by someone else. Who is that old woman looking out at me? When I first came to the boarding house, when I was told that the job was mine, I thought of shaving off the hair that I have worn long almost all of my life – shaving it off to the skull. I could get big dangly earrings, to look like, I don't know what, some kind of a gypsy, I suppose. Do you know that a gypsy woman in the north of England put a curse on my mother? She said not my mother, nor any of her offspring, would ever find rest. We would wander the face of the earth, no place to lay our heads. May be some truth in that, but for myself, I don't mind being a wanderer. What sort of a curse is that? Yes, in front of the mirror this morning I pulled back my shoulders, adjusted the angle of my jaw. Was this thin tight-lipped smile really mine? I scraped my hair back into its bun and saw as if for the first time how the deep long straight cracks of white hair cut through the heavy brown pulled tight around my skull. I have given up that idea of changing my looks. After what has happened now, after Herbert's death, it does not seem right to draw attention to myself. After such a death, it can seem audacious, even, to comb one's hair.

This morning it was the state of my eyes that struck me most forcibly. There in the mirror, my eyes, yes, they were framed by their crow's-feet, most deep and crowding out everything else when I smiled. But it is not just that – that sign of ageing is to be expected. No, what I saw in the mirror was how the composition of the eyes themselves had changed, how their luminosity seemed spent. I hoped that it was just the sorrow.

3

When the chorea had first started, Herbert used to think of it as having its origins deep within him, as if some inner truth that wanted release, a small piece of him disgruntled with the body and its constraints, straining to be free. Not any longer. Here in Doornfontein Hospital, Herbert can no sooner contain the sweeping flitting of his extremities as a newly revolving windmill can stop its blind broken churning against the wind. He has come to understand that the chorea comes from outside him, like the wind, not from within. The visit to my sweat-shop and what had happened there fades in and out of Herbert's consciousness. Just as when he had set out one day to find a sulphur spring – the one that he had wished to show me – however hard he walked, he could not find it. The nurses tell Herbert that he has had enough excitement in his life and that he should stay indoors and rest. Herbert does not like to rest. It is then that the movements of his body start up in earnest. Even now, even in this early morning in the hospital, Herbert has to put an elbow firmly on his thigh to try to stop the thigh from thumping, and, with it, his body bumping against the iron bedstead. He sits. His chorea helps him to disentangle his thoughts and his thoughts are purposeful today, not like before. Everything that comes into his head is beginning to coalesce and the picture forming in his mind is like a map he cannot read. He does not give up.

Despite his frail appearance, Herbert is a strong man and he wonders if one day he might crack his own thigh bone with the strength of his elbow pushing on it. Which twig would snap first, the bone of the arm (he forgets its name) or the femur? Herbert has spent some time looking at *Henry Gray's Anatomy of the Human Body* in the nurses' office. A good heavy book – he could do with it now to weigh down his legs. In recent years, Herbert has made a study of the skeleton and the muscles and tendons that are supposed to make it work. There is not much else to do in Doornfontein. He expected that the mental exercise would keep his brain alive longer. And it has – for see, Herbert knows that the textbook, and the rest of medical science as far as he can tell, describes, but it does not explain. So there is a name to his condition – what does that tell you other than its name? A name, not even your own name, can tell you what will happen to you. If you care to look at the picture-books, the name of your condition will be there, and they will show you a picture of your brain and how it differs from someone who does not have this condition, or has another, or none at all that medical science has yet staked out as its own. No name can foretell whether or not you will find the strength to act on your desires.

There will be a bruise here on Herbert's thigh tomorrow where he has banged against the bedstead, a big purple stain, slowly turning yellow around the edges. The colours of the bruise will change even slower than a sunset, even slower than the certain darkening of the skies.

Herbert is always the first to hear the ringing of the dinner bell – breakfast, lunch and supper. There it is now. He pulls on his suit trousers as rapidly as he can, taking deep breaths, half-humming a tune.

'Riches I want not, nor man's empty praise . . .'

Herbert has always liked that song because the melody perfectly fits the timbre of his voice. But it is not just the tune that he likes; something in the words themselves reminds him of his life. It is too hot to put on the socks and shoes that Jane has put out for him. There will be plenty of time to change into those later. Instead, Herbert pulls on his open shoes, the ones that allow his feet to breathe. Before leaving his room he looks down at the fine bones of his feet. He wriggles the toes, marvelling at how the tendons stand out like small ropes. For just a moment he feels like a specimen of something fine, something well made. He straightens his back and walks steadily out into the corridor, carefully closing the door behind him.

The porridge pot has not yet arrived from the kitchen, despite the smell of it and the ringing of the bell. Herbert goes to sit in the corner of the dining room beside the fan. The arms of the fan are whirring already in anticipation of the heat. How easily one day can blur into the next. He puts his hand to his heart to touch the small wooden bottle inside his shirt pocket. Gusts of cool air brush against his eyelashes, then warm again, as the head of the fan swings away, then cool gentle fluttering once more. Back and forth, warm and cool. Herbert closes his eyes. Up on the mountainside the wide, open, cloudscudded skies blow overhead. For some people, being alone is the same as being free.

Herbert seldom receives visitors. People you know from before can always find a reason not to come to a place such as Doornfontein. And when they do come, they usually arrive with things from their world – fruit and suchlike, as if to compensate for the soul's meanness. On one occasion that I visited him, I heard Herbert pronounce that the more comfortable a person gets in their life, the more selfish they become. I still do not know if by saying that, he meant to accuse me of the same. Before his experience at the hospital, Herbert was not like that – he did not expect more than a person gave and so he was never disappointed. Something in that place corrupted him. The nurses don't like the patients to receive visitors. They say it is upsetting. I visited Herbert at least once a year. I would come with a pie tucked in my bags, or some uncomfortable shirt I had sewn, sometimes a pin still forgotten there, as if something in me still wished to hurt him, or so he thought.

'Better just to let things be,' the nurses say.

Herbert does not begrudge them. Nurses are creatures of routine. That is how they are trained.

Before he was informed that he had fathered a child, Herbert had no idea that the possibility existed. And so that day in 1933, more than ten years back now, when two women had come to see him at Doornfontein Hospital, the news they brought took him by surprise. He thinks of it now, trying to trace the pattern of their visit in his mind. It was a hot day just like this one, and early in the morning. The fan blowing warm and cool beside him now reminds him of that day.

Sister Jane had showed the two visitors in. They brought out no pies or cakes, no knitted slippers, no soap or razors.

'Mr Wakeford, do you remember Anna Papenas?' the nurse had asked him.

Why, of course he did. Why ever not? Had he not so long before, cut this Anna's hair, laughing and smiling in Sara's back garden? So Herbert smiled and laughed again just as they had that day. His laugh came out differently from what he intended, louder, more raucous, and so the girl and her mother pulled away.

Herbert saw that Anna had changed. He had seen this coming already several months back in Cape Town on his annual visit to us there – had watched as Anna's face took on an other-worldly hue, all its colours becoming muted. He could even have told the sex of the child she carried, had anyone cared to ask. Instead, after a few weeks and sensing he was no longer wanted, Herbert had left us, returned to the company of the nurses at Doornfontein and the distraction of his daily chores. And now, just a few months on, here Anna was, come to see him. Herbert pushed out his hand in greeting, swallowing the laughter rising in his throat as best he could. His hand began to jerk so he stuffed it back into his jacket pocket. With all his heart, Herbert wanted this girl to remember that day he cut her hair. So Herbert reached into his jacket pocket to pull out his scissors to remind her of that day. But there were no scissors in his pocket. They did not allow Herbert to keep scissors in the

83

hospital. Even today, it is not allowed. Herbert has no means with which to cut off the stray thread that he notices hanging from a button of his best white shirt. He knows he must not pull on it.

No matter, Herbert should not have worried about Anna forgetting him, for it soon became apparent that she recalled more than Herbert himself. He stood at attention, rapt as she spoke. Anna's mother stood beside him. The old lady's steel-grey hair was pulled tight as a helmet around her head. Anna and her mother took it in turns, helping each other out to supply every detail, every accusation. These two visitors stood alongside him with their wagging fingers and accusing tongues and papers flapping in the breeze of the fan. And so when they instructed him to, Herbert was able to sign the form. The nurse signed as witness. When it was all done to their satisfaction, Anna Papenas and her mother rose to leave. Perhaps it was then that Herbert realised that for some indeterminate period, his chorea had been stilled.

'Don't go. Come and walk with me in the hospital gardens.'

But they looked at Herbert as if he had lost his marbles. Then they picked their way down the embankment, just as they had come up. They walked jerkily, a little like the walking in the Charlie Chaplin movies shown in the dining room last Christmas Day.

Many other things that happened to Herbert over the years that followed were soon lost to his mind, but the news that Miss and Mrs Papenas brought Herbert that day so long ago – news that he, Herbert Wakeford had begotten a child, this information burrowed deep inside him, and once there, it refused to give up its home. And Abraham begot Isaac, and Isaac begot Jacob, and Jacob . . . And Herbert Wakeford rolled around the names of those begot in the hospital wards, driving his fellow patients crazy with his choice of names. He felt open as the sky. This child would be free.

Sister Jane had been the only sister on duty that day. She had helped with the paperwork and she told Herbert that the Lord would provide. She had not seemed angry with him. The nurse at least would be his friend.

He was not present at the birth. A month later the child was deposited on the front lawn of the hospital gardens, a small soft blue oval tucked neatly into a wooden apple crate. Herbert stood at the window of the dining room of Doornfontein Hospital and watched the retreating backs of the Papenases once again, heading down the slope, and once again he laughed. When no one that mattered was about, Herbert set that laugh free from the prison of his mind. He laughed aloud and he laughed again and he did not try to make the laughter civilised, for that would have silenced the laughter and there would have been no more left. Jake Hangklip stood beside him. This was the man who was incarcerated at Doornfontein because he had long ago murdered his wife with a pickaxe. Which does not explain why Jake was having a holiday here and not doing time in jail, building roads and suchlike. After Anna and her mother had disappeared from view, Jake stepped outside. He looked down at the little infant lying on the lawn in its bundle, much as a person might view a corpse. Then he picked up the soft oval mass, slung it workmanlike over his shoulder and, seemingly oblivious to its sudden fretfulness, strolled over to the nurses' common room.

'It's tired,' Jake said. 'Find the mite some place to rest.'

Herbert has never been sure that he could tell someone who has lost their marbles from a common criminal. Seems that some folks think that they can. What is it to be good? Why are some not held accountable for what they do, while others are? So much about this life that he does not understand. Still, he likes Jake, all the same.

That year of 1934, the first year of Aloma Maggie's life, Herbert Wakeford was the envy of all in Doornfontein. Much to the nurses' horror, he received visitors every single weekend.

Each Sunday afternoon he stepped out into the Karoo sunshine to greet Mrs Agnes Booysen and her husband. The pair of them came as if strung together with laces, their faces twinned in anxiety. These were the foster paupers that Sister Jane found to help with his baby. They came each week. They brought his daughter Maggie to show Herbert that the child was still living and to collect the small change he could offer from his savings in return for her keep. Mrs Booysen cocked her head this way and that, informing Herbert about the rash, the sleepless nights, the washing of the nappies, and later, the carelessness of the child, the broken goods. Her eyes were pleading shifty beads and her talk was guarded.

The fan blows back and forth now, warm and cool as Herbert Wakeford sits in the hospital dining room. 'I would that you were either hot or cold,' the Scriptures say. 'But because you are lukewarm I will spew you out of my mouth.'

Some priest at Jane's church had spoken these words the previous Sunday. Herbert liked the sound that the words made as they fell against his brain. He thought that he knew their meaning without being told, much as you may think that you know the meaning of a foreign language, when accompanied by gestures, by the ringing of a bell.

Later he had told Jane that the porridge at Doornfontein comes neither hot nor cold. The staff say that it is the patients' fault if the porridge is lukewarm but this is nonsense. Look, the porridge pot has not yet arrived in the dining room and Herbert is here already, waiting.

That first year of Maggie's life was the last year of Herbert's walking without aid. Herbert and Maggie passed the baton sometime that year – her walk began to strengthen as his began to falter. By the time that she was able to walk up towards the hospital entrance, her fat hand holding Mrs Booysen's flowered dress, Herbert could not count on being able to come out to greet them without his walking stick. Leaning on his stick, he steered his child and her carers into the hospital dining room. There, where she could pull on a tablecloth upsetting a pot of tea and breaking the china. Neither Herbert nor Mrs Booysen was fast enough to stop her. By Maggie's second birthday, Herbert's strength began to spew out in uncontrollable directions. It would have been easier, he thought, if the strength was sapped from him, as his child became stronger, but that was not how it happened

– it was, in fact, the opposite. Walking across the plate of the earth, he feared that he would break the earth itself with his chorea.

I know now that in those first years of Maggie's life, more than once Herbert tried to set out to call on me, but weak with influenza, or exhausted from lack of sleep, he could not ascend the first koppie. The porters came and carried him, floppy as any wilted carrot, home.

'A danger to himself and others,' the doctors said.

Herbert had no choice but to believe them, for he heard no other voices. And so he did not fight it when they took away his key to the hospital building. And he did not fight it, not right away, when the nurses insisted he start to use a wheelchair.

'You may as well get used to it,' they said. 'You will be unable to walk soon enough, you know.'

At first Herbert humoured them. He sat in the chair and thick white calluses formed on his palms where they made contact with its steel wheels. Thin white scars like flattened worms rested on his fingers where they caught on the wheels' spokes. Yet all along Herbert did not want to be locked in, nor did he wish for confinement in a chair. To Herbert, his march across the face of the earth has always been like the flowing of the blood in the body, the proof of his being alive.

Herbert was certain that I would come to him. But I would not. I had no desire to see him after hearing of the birth of his child. Cora came instead, Cora Rynhardt. When Herbert saw Cora's teetering walk up through the short brown winter of the grass, he knew that this was Maggie's chance for a better kind of a life. And so Herbert forgot for a moment that his wheelchair was a prison and a shame, and he rolled out to meet Cora. Herbert saw too late that he was without doubt about to tumble chair and all down the slope in full view of the occupants of the dining room. Cora caught a-hold of his chair, digging her high heels into the clay earth to support them both. And so that was how Herbert Wakeford and Cora Rynhardt clung to one another in front of the picture window of Doornfontein Hospital. This was the final proof that Herbert needed – evidence that Cora was quick enough to look after the child. He had witnesses. Cora would be the nursemaid and Sara the mother, he decided. And so that day a small green shoot of Herbert's hope came out, a small uprising in his harsh Namaqua desert.

For some time after that, Herbert refused to sit in his wheelchair.

'If you do not use your talents, they will be taken away from you,' he told the nurses.

They could not argue with the Scriptures and so they let him be. Victorious, Herbert regained his strength.

He takes his breakfast bowl now up to the pink lady. This lady, this little bird with the glasses, always serves bigger portions to those patients at the front of the line. Perhaps this is to encourage the patients to come on time to their meals. Herbert is almost always first. He remembers to tuck his serviette under his chin so as not to mess on his clothes. When Herbert has finished his breakfast he makes his way to the bathroom. He has eaten without spilling on his suit, just as he had promised Jane that he would.

* * * *

Thinking of Herbert spilling food on his clothes reminds me of his child – for she, like Herbert, seemed to need a bib or a towel draped across her clothes, long after the usual age. Some children are like that – genuinely clumsy. When I had first heard the news that Herbert and Anna's child had been born, I could not help myself crowing. A girl, Aloma Margaret Proctor. Aloma Margaret! Well, Margaret was a respectable sort of a name, but Aloma! Where had Herbert unearthed such a name?

Cora pronounced each month that the child would now give a recognisable smile, may have said her first word, and she wondered what it was. Probably sitting up now, for yes she was around nine months old, and so on, nine or perhaps ten, we were not quite sure, walking, talking. At that time we did not know the colour of the child's eyes or her hair, or who cared for her. Knew only that she lived somewhere close by to her father, and that he made her first pair of little shoes with his own hand, of canvas, soled with old cycle tyres. One day Cora travelled to Doornfontein Hospital to see how Herbert and his child were getting along.

'How is the child, Cora? Is she healthy?'

Cora shook her head so that her spectacles dropped to the floor. She bent over like a thin crooked pin to pick them up.

'The money,' she said. 'They are demanding from Herbert more money than he can provide.'

Cora started up a collection in the Presbyterian Church, any old clothes, any old toys, these would all be put to good use.

'And how did you find his child? Does the babe look at all like her father?'

'Oh yes,' Cora declared. 'Peas in a pod. I just can't understand how any mother would walk away from a bonny child like that.'

And when a few months had passed, around the time of the child's fourth birthday, I said to Cora to go back to Doornfontein. I prepared a small gift. There would be no harm in it. I made up a small sewing set. Wound some coloured threads onto cardboard tares, a red, a yellow, an orange and a pink. Wrapped in a paper two thick darning needles that a child could learn to handle. Sewed a little bag to hold the needles and threads, one that rolled and secured with a bright green ribbon. Embroidered her initials A.M.P. for decoration, and it was all done. Did not bother with a card. Not for her, a child that age too young to read, she would just toss a card aside.

Cora Rynhardt settled into the second class carriage, her bags at her feet. She had plenty of luggage. She clutched a return ticket and tucked beneath her arm, a small box of food for the journey.

I always knew that Cora Rynhardt did not approve of my affair with the Indian Quality Controller because of Hafferjee's marriage, and also because he was Indian. You could not help but see the cloud pass across her face whenever Hafferjee was near. Yet it was whilst Cora was visiting Herbert and his child at Doornfontein Hospital that Hafferjee and I parted ways.

But first, since I was alone in the house, Hafferjee came to stay for a weekend. I suppose he thought that this would please me. Despite the modern ideal of intimacy, it is my belief that too much closeness creates its own unnecessary difficulties.

Hafferjee was curled up loosely on my bed as if he belonged there. All at once, he pulled a photograph out from where he had it hidden beside his chest. He passed it over to me with a certain formality, as if he wished me to take it seriously. It is polite to look at a picture that someone shows you. So I brought it within the arc of the lamplight and held it up to get a better view. It was a professional sort of a job: Hafferjee and his teenage sons wore a white smock apiece, collars starched. Each had a different pattern embroidered on either side of the smock's flat cleavage. Hafferjee, the upright, flanked by two boys. He sported a single white carnation pinned on the embroidery where the lapel hole would have been, had he been wearing tails and not a smock. The dark hair and wistful look of a wife and mother were placed in the centre of the picture. They were not smiling into the camera, not one, but looking straight ahead. I passed back the picture hastily. That is how people dress, I told myself in panic. That is how people dress, formal-like. People wear these clothes, it is just a costume. It is respectable, Sara, I told myself. It is just respectable.

But I could not help crying out.

'Why white! A white carnation! Do not bring pictures of white flowers into this here house! Don't you know white flowers bring bad luck? White flowers bring death,' I told Hafferjee. 'You should never have brought that picture of a stiff white flower into this house.'

And so I showed Hafferjee the door and I said that he should never return. There was no ambiguity. And as I said it, I felt I was bringing misfortune on myself simply by the saying of it. After all, a man who wears a white carnation in his lapel hole, what sort of a man is this?

For years afterwards I tried to tease my body into remembering Amin Hafferjee but it would not be stirred. Yet because it has been so before, I cannot help but wonder if one day again, the river may flood. When Amin Hafferjee arrived at the boarding house today, he came bearing fruit. This was all the more precious for being scarce, for during the autumn, after the summer fruits and before the citrus, there is nothing at all to be found in the shops. Hafferjee, being a tenacious sort of a man, had hunted the shelves until he found the apples. Three over-priced, shrivelled-up fruits. He brought them in a small brown paper bag, clutched it to his chest. They sit now on the corner of my desk. After all these years and having heard of my recent loss, Hafferjee still knew better than to bring me flowers.

After what happened that day with the picture, I decided that I could not, with a clear conscience, take Hafferjee's business again. I suppose I could have found other contracts to take its place, but something in my heart would not allow it. It was time to move on. Cora, having always lived in Cape Town, would have tried to dissuade me. I had moved before and I knew that I could welcome the change. It was easier to keep my resolve with Cora away. I began to make the necessary arrangements.

If one must move, it is always a little easier to go somewhere familiar and so I decided on Brakpan. The little white mine house with the picket fence to keep in the goats had long since been allocated to another compound manager. So I wrote to Frank and Sybil. They had stayed on all those years, had bought a plot a little way out of town and there on his own piece of land, Frank had built a house by floodlight, painting each new room a different colour so that no one would get lost. Frank was a good correspondent, the pictures of his life in his letters as colourful and ramshackle as his building projects. Their house was too big for just the two of them, he said, and they were looking to take in boarders. He seemed to be expecting me.

Eight years since I last lived here in Cape Town. The mountain shadow keeps the light from too much brightness, and in summer, the South-Easter's relentless gusts seem to take something unsettled and rootless in those who live here, and write it larger. The North-Wester blows in the autumn, even the shadows cast by the clouds feel cold. It has begun to rain today. The first of the autumn rains come far too early. Floss Streuban, back from her hairdressing appointment, came in just now to complain that the fireplace in the lounge is leaking, smoking every time you try to light a fire. She had a good look at Hafferjee, waited for an introduction. Meddlesome old bird, some days I longed to pierce that ancient scalp with a hairpin. Raining again, just like the day of Cora's return from Doornfontein Hospital so long ago.

The day I expected Cora back, I rose early so as to be ready to meet her. It was raining just like it is today. The station platform was already busy when I arrived. Muddy self-important footprints merged, coming and going into a thin film of sludge at the ticket office. I stood motionless on the tile I had selected on the platform, a place with good sight of the line where the carriages would stop. The platform began to tremble with the noise of the approaching train. People surged forward to take their places close to the line. A child shrieked, the clatter of a suitcase's metal strappings, a phrase of an argument, another's embrace. Part of me, I could have sworn, was pushed away in a shiny trolley by a uniformed man, on down that platform. Oh! But there. Cora's anxious wave appeared through the window of the carriage. Her hand stopped fluttering as she focused on tottering on down the corridor towards the door.

The first thing that I saw emerge from the door of that carriage was a stuffed animal, a knitted thing, pink and grubby. Then Cora's strappy shoes, the black straps pinching her pale ankles, puffy and mottled from the journey. She seemed to have found herself a travelling companion, for next, between the legs of the other disembarking passengers, a podgy arm, the arm of a small child, holding Cora's dress. The two of them began picking their way over to where I stood. As they came closer, Cora did not take her eyes off my face. With her free hand she clutched the upper arm of the child, as if afraid she would try to run away. Even as I looked around for the child's mother, I knew she would not be seen. A new kind of fate was rolling its wheels towards me. Surely this thing had gone far enough.

'Sara,' Cora said, embracing me with her awkward fluster.

My brogues were as if cast in stone on the platform. I did not sway in the breeze.

'Sar, I am pleased to introduce Miss Aloma Maggie

95

Proctor. Maggie.' Cora stooped conspiratorially to the child, as people do when they think a child can understand. 'Maggie,' she said, 'this lady is your auntie. Auntie Sara Highbury.'

The child fought free of Cora's grip and leapt at me as a monkey might to its mother. She was a child expecting to be welcomed, with a child's sense of entitlement; she expected an embrace, took her embrace from me. I had no choice in it. I, who did not wish to stop her.

'So this is Maggie,' I said. And what brings you here, child? What right have you to be turning up here without invitation in the Cape?

The girl, in her features, and her body, its hard round high-set paunch that pushed her pelvis forwards so that she looked off-kilter, though with a child's ease with herself, she looked like nothing I knew. She could have been anyone.

We walked across the platform. Along the way Cora fluttered off with much muttering and fluster of handbag and rearranging of baggage, to relieve herself. The child held my hand for a little, then dropped it, and dragged her heels. A little later, I looked down to find that Miss Aloma Maggie had already fallen back. There, further down the platform, the child stood, motionless, staring up at the large station clock mounted on the high wide lintel ahead, above the ticket office. Her neck acutely angled upwards. Even from this distance, I could make out the movement of the child's eyes following the tick tick tick of the thin second hand, ratcheting in a slow-motion arc around the clock face. Seeing her thus, I recalled Herbert, the day we had first met, a rainy day the same, seeing him stand, water draining off him, and his eyes fixed on the distant church steeple, transfixed, the set of his mouth, his matchstick limbs, the way he had of standing, feet apart, and swaying slightly, swaying as if held together like some kind of insect, a praying mantis I had thought then, the kind of an insect that brings a blessing. This girl had black eyes. For a moment I could not remember the colour of Herbert's eyes. I focused my mind, and what appeared was Herbert's silhouette in the house in Bloemhof, moving about here and there in his stuttering, jerky kind of way. I tried harder, and caught the feel of his hips against my own walking across the veld, here then gone. Herbert was gone.

I don't know why it is that I recall the incident of the rat so well. I suppose it is because that is the first time that I heard Maggie laugh.

As we were walking home from the station, a rat ran across the wet and puddled street. Its tail disappeared through a gap in a wall. Aloma Maggie released her grip on my fingers and jumped the few paces to the rat hole to investigate. Seconds later, she leapt back in surprise. The rat was reversing out of the gap, its tail first. Behind it was another rat, teeth bared. The first was shrieking from between its teeth, gripping a crust of bread. When they saw Maggie standing there, the rats forgot their differences, turned tail and disappeared. Without any warning or signal, Aloma Maggie laughed. Later those who knew her would be alerted by the twitch of her shoulders, the twitch that always preceded the laugh, a signal if you knew to look for it. A deep throaty laugh, working up into a snort like an angry pig guffawing for its food, a small explosion. The laugh was quite out of character with Maggie's shyness, her laugh was twice the volume of her voice, but not a high-pitched nervous shriek, it was deep and weighty, too weighty for a child. Then I believed that this, Aloma Maggie Proctor, was indeed Herbert's child. And she should be carrying Herbert's name, not the name of . . . whose name was this that she carried? Was this the name of some mad woman in Doornfontein Hospital, for lack of a father to acknowledge her?

This child wore stiff new clothes. Not like Herbert – his trousers were loose, like the robes of Christ himself, the fabric was soft, as if softened by love for his body. There was something artificially groomed about his child's white-frilled shirt and blue skirt to her knees. Must be a woman involved, and I knew it was not Cora, for she would not have had the money then. I should have run a mile, seeing the clothes, but I didn't. What stopped me were Maggie's shoes, for these, it seemed to me then, told the truth. Over her white flimsy socks, the child wore sandals of sagging canvas, like miniature versions of Herbert's shoes, and soled by the same thin bony hand with old cycle tyres. Herbert and his child, they wore their strongest bond in their footprints.

I saw all these things, but as hard as I tried to remember him, I could not see a picture of the whole man. Images and fragments fell into a new kaleidoscope pattern each time the child threw up her arms to remark on this thing or that.

'Stop!' I heard myself yelling. 'Stop her! That child is about to run into the path of a carriage! Stop!'

But it was I who caught her, just in time. I congratulated myself for being spared the undue expense of doctor's bills to set a broken arm, and all the tears and hullabaloo that would have gone with it. I had already been snared by then, was well on my way to becoming domesticated through the rise and fall of anxieties and relief, about this and that little thing to do with Maggie's welfare.

That night, after supper, between Cora's incessant chatter, a silence fell on us. Aloma lay in a crumpled heap, mouth open, collapsed on the floor, marking the place she deigned to fall. Cora carried the child to rest more comfortably on my bed. Said she hoped Maggie would not fall out in the night. I said that I hoped that she would, for then I would have a place to lay my head. Together we folded a small blanket on the floor beside the bed to soften a fall, just in case.

Within minutes Cora was snoring in the next bed, the room cluttered and full of bodies. Aloma Maggie's little leather suitcase and shoes, and clothes and things of the house that bore the mark of her handling lay disordered all about us. I knew that this was part of the disorientation that children use to subdue adults and I resolved to keep my head. I would not be subdued by a mere child, a child I owed nothing to. I walked to the kitchen, where I sat alone at the table, and waited for morning to come.

Maggie's African-born hands were darker than mine had ever been. I suppose that many white children here are like this, owing to the sun. The soft white hands from the winters of my own childhood would have been foreign to Herbert's child, like a new kind of plant or animal she had never seen. I recall how I had splayed out my hands and traced the outline of my fingers onto newspaper with a crayon. That must have been the year I learned to write. It seems like another world now – Sunderland, north-east England. In the winter, my hands had been encased in gloves cut off at the fingers, which makes the pencil slip, but not too much, and still my hands were as warm as honey.

'Like a chimney-sweep child,' my mother had laughed, and Northumbria's cold fingers had waved me goodbye at the gate.

Later that same day my mother had been carried out of the house, a white sheet over her face like the sacraments, that morning with the fresh, soft rain, so soft on my face I could barely feel it. Fragments of my life appeared in front of my eyes in this fashion and all of these became more real to me the day that Maggie came – our time at the diggings, the anticipation of finding a stone, the way you could not get the dirt out from under your fingernails, and in Pilgrim's Rest, the grey streaked with gold, veldspar exposed by the rains still glinting in the sun. And the gold and coal mines of the Reef, the picket fences, mine dances, the flash clothes – cravats, pinstripes and shiny shoes – worn by the new bosses from London and Johannesburg, the smell of garlic and red wine, the miners' remedy to take away the boils. None of these things were of any relevance to this child, still mean nothing to her – just a small piece of history, Herbert's and mine – so dusty and uncomfortable that I am the only one who recalls them now.

I gave my notice to Pauline Kraemer. Cora would go to stay with her sister in Constantia. It was all settled more or less. As for Maggie, I must take her back to her father at Doornfontein, I said. The truth was that I knew already that I would keep the child with me, if Herbert allowed it. I would take care of her, but not here in the Cape, and not with Cora.

The night before leaving Cape Town, I did not sleep at all. I hoped to leave early, so as to avoid the awkwardness of Cora's farewell. I busied myself packing a food parcel for the train in the darkened kitchen with sandwiches, coffee, more bread. Then I put water on to boil for a final cup of tea. Whilst waiting for the kettle's song, I fingered the firm oily skin of an orange left lying on the table. I packed the orange, and a few extra tins of beans. In the end, owing to my anxieties, I was so weighed down with boxes and bags that I decided to call a horse and cart to ride to the station, and so I had to part with the first of my precious coins. It was still dark when the driver stopped by the house, the stars only just beginning to fade. Aloma Maggie lay sleeping on my bed. She had moved in the night, so that she was lying widthways, curled up, the rest of the bed's expanse unoccupied. I took a deep breath, and hoisted her sleeping form over my shoulder. I was surprised how easily I could collapse her body against my chest, and how she accepted the dangling of her arm in mid-air with hardly a sigh. In sleep she seemed to have lost all inhibition, all resistance. And yet her weight against my body told me she had developed supernatural powers of gravity, to weigh her here, as if to compensate for her life's uncertainties. How she depended on me, whilst her body seemed to believe she could find support in the air itself, with no need of other bolsters. I walked across to the front gate with my cargo, careful not to stumble and wake her. Then the driver took her from me, and laid her on an old blanket he had folded up, in a crevice between the boxes. I reassured myself that she was well wedged in. Together we wrapped a further blanket around her, its thin translucent coat of grey horsehairs shining by the light of the lantern still lit. I climbed up beside the driver, and we were off down the road with a shudder.

As we neared the end of the street, it took all the strength I could find not to look back at the house that had been my home for seven years; not to look back to see if I may catch a glimpse of a silhouette in the kitchen window. Perhaps a wave. But I did not look back.

We stopped at the station as close to the platform as was allowed. I carried the child from the cart onto the train, and loaded on our bags and boxes. She did not wake. In her sleep she clung to me, oblivious to how her bony knees and elbows jabbed me all about. I pushed her around a little to try to get more comfortable. After a while the clunk clunk of the carriage as it passed the joins in the line seemed to calm her and I lay her down with her head in my lap and her feet tucked up against the window. The line snaked through the cuttings at

Worcester, the shadow of the Devil's Peak far behind. We left the furthest reach of a vast continent, the only way out, north, hemmed in by water every which way, and rings of mountainsides, their sweet-smelling fynbos clutching at our passing. Where am I, Sara Highbury, in all of this? I do not see myself.

Some time into the morning, Aloma woke with her face flushed with heat. She smiled and began her relentless chatter.

'What happens at the mines, Sara? Why do people go there?'

'For gold, child. And other things. To get the gold.'

'Show me some. Show me the gold.'

'One day,' I told her. 'If you are good.'

Maggie settled back into her seat and within minutes fell into sleep again, rocked side by side by the motion of the train.

She woke some way into the morning with more questions crowding her head: 'A child doesn't change into another thing, Auntie Sar? Like a mouse, a lion? That's just in stories, isn't it?'

'You will never change into an elephant, you have my word. You cannot change into anything.'

'But I will turn into a grown-up one day? I will turn into that, won't I?'

'God willing, if you do as you are told and work hard at school.'

'I don't want to be a grown-up, not ever.' Maggie began to cry.

'You are a child, first a child, then much later after that a grown-up and that is that,' I said. 'I don't want to hear any more of this, be quiet now and have a rest.'

As the warmth of the sun shone through the carriage window, we shed our sun-prickled cardigans. And then whilst the wheels of the train kept their relentless turning and Maggie's cardigan lay beside her on the leather of the seat, everything changed. There across the child's soft arms for all to see sat telltale pick-pock scars, plotting a destiny, and telling of a past, on her skin's fresh parchment.

'Who did this to you, Maggie?'

Maggie has never answered that question satisfactorily – not then, nor in all the years I knew her. I don't think that she remembers now, so I wouldn't bother to ask again.

She shrugged her shoulders and looked out of the window. I took a quick and furtive study of Maggie's face. I thought then that I would find the truth somehow, in a sidelong sort of a way, as one should deal with a child, this was how to do it. Who knew where she came from, a child with no family, born out of wedlock? But still I knew, having seen this, I could not send a child not yet six years old back from whence she had come.

'Your father is not an easy man, Maggie,' I said later.

Maggie was silent for a long time. The train started a shudder shudder shudder as it pulled around a curve in the line. Perhaps she was considering some other thing, a doll perhaps or toy she wanted, much more pressing for a child.

'I once saw a dead person,' she announced. 'Long time ago.'

She fell back into thinking. I wondered what she saw

when she recalled death, and what Herbert's child had seen of life. He used to speak of the living, saying that some of us may as well be dead. He liked to speak of the difference between the living and the dead in strange ways – something to do with the strength of the gaze was his favourite. We sat in silence for a while longer until Maggie spoke again.

'Are we going to Bloemhof?' she asked. 'My dad says that is the best place in the world. I'd like to live at the diggings, Sara. Please take me there, please.'

'The diggings are no place for a child. Why, I know of a man who dug over his own mother's grave to search for stones. And another who tunnelled under his house and was buried alive beneath it when the tunnel collapsed, his wife and children watching. They are a rough sort of person there. Your father wants you brought up proper and decent.'

'I can help look for stones. I have sharp eyes.'

'The machinery is too heavy for us girls,' I said at last.

I wished to say to her that if Herbert gets better and out of hospital, we could all go together to Bloemhof and gather a few stones from God's earth. Looking back now, of course, I see that it was always meant to be that Maggie and I would go north together, but not to Bloemhof; I would not take the child to the diggings. What if the diamond fever overtook her? What if, like Herbert, she lost her marbles?

Frank and Sybil's house was, just as they said, much too big for the two of them. But the children they tried for night after night refused to stick it out in Sybil's hostile womb. Frank dug trenches to water the vegetables and big bright dahlias and pansies for a while, to be viewed from the kitchen window. One of his hobbies was fixing cars and so in time he tossed out the broken shells of a few old Austins where in the yard their crippled rusty bodies broke and bruised stems and unsuspecting succulent leaves. Maggie and I had the sole use of the blue room, and the yellow, and shared the kitchen and the outside bathroom, but we had our own entrance, our own front door. We slept in the blue room. I used the yellow room for sewing, taking in orders for the ladies, wedding outfits, dresses for a ball or a christening. This was high art, not contracts. It was important always to speak well to the ladies, and to reassure them that the designs were flattering, as well as sensible, to put them at their ease.

My first order in Brakpan was for a wedding. Mrs Plunkett and her daughter and the two cousins came for their dress fittings on a Saturday afternoon. Mrs Plunkett had a sensible suit in navy, broad lapels, three-quarter sleeves, a hat to match with a sort of a veil attached. She stood in her baize petticoat, rolled over lumpily at the waist as it was too long. A musty smell of old stocking blew towards the door. She climbed onto the table, her strapped ankles threatening to collapse beneath her. I drew the curtain lest Frank come home early from the shift. Aloma Maggie hoisted the mirror up onto the table as I pinned the pleats. I soon forgot Hafferjee and all that had passed between us in Cape Town; until his visit today, it was almost as if it had never happened.

At Maggie's behest, I suggested Frank close up the

106

door between our rooms and theirs with planks. I could not help wondering where this desire had come from, if there had been a happening in her past. Frank was not offended that she should wish to barricade them out.

'She's entitled to her opinion, Sara,' he said.

That night Frank told us how a man once took the trouble to lip-print a thousand cows.

'Amongst a thousand cows, each one produced a different lip print, not a single print the same. Just like humans. We are all different. It is only our education, and our culture, that makes us appear the same.'

Maggie never forgot that tale, she reminded me of it many times as she grew older, as if she forgot I had heard it too. Frank did not get around to putting up the barricade, and Aloma did not ask again. Whatever troubled her blew over.

We enrolled Maggie in the English-speaking school in Brakpan. I filled out the form. I pronounced myself the mother, and our residential address, Plot 481, Brakpan. I lacked the birth certificate, and I lacked proof of Maggie's health and hygiene. Still because they could see that Maggie was clever and would not be any trouble, the school took her in. I received a warning, however.

'The documents must be provided, madam. It is a requirement of the Board of Education.'

I suppose I thought then that these requirements too would simply blow over one day like a child's concerns, cease to be of any significance.

Those years we lived with them I saw more than I wished of Frank and Sybil's union. Wondered if this was how a marriage was, or if like the cow's lip prints,

each one was different. Frank expected Maggie's coop-
eration. He signalled her more than once to take jars
of Marmalade, Peach Preserve, Lemon Curd from the
shelf above the sink. These had at one time or another
bubbled for days on the stove outside and then been
poured and sealed. They were Sybil's pride, second
only to her sewing.

'Here, put these jars outside the back door, they can
as well lie there as take up the shelf space. Come on,
lend a hand here.' He squeezed Maggie's arm as if he
knew she'd need some of his strength to do it. 'We
shouldn't eat this stuff,' he declared. 'Rots the teeth.'

Then Frank showed the child, wide open like a
sponge, drinking up his every word, how to sort and
fill new jars from a drum of scraps and rubbish, mixed
up. Masonry nails, panel pins, long nails, short nails,
match the bolts and nuts, a good three twists the male
to the female. He put a sample of each type in a jar.
Later, these displays of order would stand proudly on
the kitchen shelf, a shelf now full of useful things.
Cutlery tipped from the drawer, its compartments too
well suited to spanners and screwdrivers, so these took
the place of the knives and forks. Now a person would
know exactly where to find a thing, if they were looking
for it. Sybil thudded about the house, swinging her
arms as if to marching orders as she walked. She
slammed the blackened cast-iron frying pan onto the
table, pushed food in Frank's direction, closed doors
with a greater force than the act of closing required.
Maggie was this extra limb to Frank. She went along
with it, because – I don't know why, just because she
allowed herself to be carried by the weight of expec-

tation, the way a child is wont to do. I had not seen this clearly at the time. Not that seeing or understanding a thing helps a person intervene. Sometimes a person just knows what to do, or does it without seeing.

All miners drink a lot. It is the way they wash the taste of the mine out of their mouths. Frank was no exception, and only once, it bothered me. I knew, of course, how slippery liquor can be, if left to flow unchecked, but with Frank, it was not a serious matter, not at that time, in any case. I am thinking of that day in Brakpan when a fine commotion came from the back yard of our house. Heard raised voices I did not at first recognise. Maggie was nowhere to be seen. Missing all morning, heavens knows where she walked off to now, had been disappearing too much lately, I must put a stop to it.

'No, no, no, no.'

Some agitated mutters, murmurs, anger and disdain. Oh yes, that was Sybil's mumble, no mistaking it now. And Frank's impatience. Who am I to interfere, if a man and a woman be working something out? Sounds of a scuffle, a chair falling. A shot cracked the air, and at this I jumped up and ran to investigate.

Frank stood at the back door. He stepped out towards me as I came around the side of the house, his .410 shotgun at rest across his forearm. He looked at me and pretended to pull the trigger. Ignoring his cockiness, I pushed past him, and stepped up inside.

'What is going on here?'

The room was momentarily black until my eyes adjusted from the bright outside light. Sybil was crouched on the floor, sleeves rolled. Face reddened. Water dripping across her forearms, one hand holding the bucket's rim, the scrubbing brush on the floor beside, face screwed tighter than the cloth she was using to wipe the washed floor dry.

'What in heaven's name is going on here? Is it over now? Are you sure it is over?'

Frank stood on the top step, the gun too close to his thigh. That shotgun could kill at fifty paces. Sybil was always on to him to get rid of it: 'Too dangerous these days with kids about the place,' she had said.

Frank's voice was still raised, something self-righteous in the tone, something not yet completely tamed. 'Couple of buck grazing on the peas out in the garden. I provided some discouragement. The woman couldn't take it.' Frank spat into the dust beside the step.

Sybil looked up, bristling. If she were called to start the fight again, she would, she would not budge, pushed up her sleeves still further in anticipation. 'They are my peas,' she hissed. 'They are my peas.'

She turned towards me.

'He mustn't, I said he mustn't shoot. Those are my peas. Let the animals eat them if they must. There is plenty for all. And if there are not enough, I will just plant again.'

The crack of another shot brought my eyes to the tears at their rims. Sybil did not flinch. As Frank came into the house, his eyes met mine beneath the door's lintel as if it was obvious that I should have a judgement on this, and that it would be in his favour; he looked to me for an opinion. I did not know. He turned away, shrugged his shoulders then pushed past me,

110

on his way to walk down the passage. But not before I saw the slight shudder of his arm's motion as he tossed the shotgun to one side on the floor, and his clockwork sway that told me to look past his grimacing face to see the clouds of Klipdrift brandy floating there, the golden liquor he loved to pour, clouding the skies of his eyes. While Sybil, like Herbert, did not touch a drop and wore the white ribbon, its silent preaching trying to shame the rest of us, there was nothing at all I could read in her eyes. They were all closed over. I'd rather have a cloud or two than that, I thought. When Frank had left, Sybil calmed.

'I know he meant no harm, has had a bit to drink, but look at it my way. What if a child were playing out at the back?' A sharp frown cut across her forehead so that she winced. Then she turned away from me and recommenced her scrubbing.

'Leave the buck. Peas can always be planted again. They are my peas.'

Then, still without looking up . . . 'Where is Aloma?'

I ran out down the steps across the yard to where the trellis of creeper climbed the fencing rigged up between two creosote poles. Those lovely sweet small peas. Could picture Aloma sitting eating them, straight from the pods. Just the kind of thing the child would do. Perhaps the buck had not visited at all, the tugging of the vines been Aloma all along.

'Maggie Aloma; Maggie, are you here?'

But no answer.

No body lying there, so she must be safe. A few small hoof prints, evidence of the buck's visitation. I went back inside.

Sybil was still muttering under her breath.

'I told him to let that buck eat the peas. I will just plant again.'

Then from the front window I heard a voice calling me.

'Sara. Sara. Here I am.'

As I came out, a peach-stone hit me on the head.

'Pow, pow,' called a voice, and a giggle.

'Get down. You'll fall out from that tree, break your neck. Get inside this minute. Give Sybil some help now, she's washing the floor on her own. Stop dragging your feet, Aloma, you'll wear out your shoes before their time.'

And so the girl grew around us, fitting into our crevices, Frank, Sybil and me, adapting herself to our foibles. We were old, powerless, like rocks, you could not move us, set in this way, the child's vines twisted and gnarled all about. Yes, it was with horror I watched this, the way Aloma grew. Because of what that doctor had said about Herbert so long ago, because of the illness passed down through the family, I did not think that her future would be bright.

One evening Maggie brought out her first school project. A blank sheet of paper she had been given, instructed to provide her Family Tree.

'No such thing,' I said. 'Families are nothing like a tree. Make a web,' I advised. 'A spider's web of names, places, gaps through which to fall, things we know nothing about. Some hapless creatures caught in between.'

'But I have to make a tree of it, Auntie Sara,' she complained.

Eventually I suggested she make herself the trunk, and

all the rest, the branches. And Cora and others who were not so connected, they all were minor twigs out at the edges of the page.

Cora visited us there in Brakpan once or twice. She got along well with Frank – he has always been popular with the ladies.

* * * *

This boarding house was once long ago occupied by a family. Hard to think of it now as a family home. This was before the bigger rooms were partitioned off, with 'cardboard', as the tenants insist upon describing it. The old man in Room 42, Mr Saus, told me yesterday that he can hear Mrs Phoebe Joubert and her husband in 44 grunting and grinding away rhythmically night after night. With one screaming baby already, Mr Saus thought that they would have learned their lesson. His old thick fingers sorted through the coins in the depths of his trouser pockets, as if half hoping they might combust, but he will never visit the girls down on the other end of the street with the red lights in their windows. No he will not. And then there is Robert Silverstein. He threads his way through the chairs to his favourite beside the window, and he will not rise again until supper. He has watered-down eyes like mine, the kind that before ageing would have been acid blue.

There is one small window here alongside my desk, so small as to scarcely be worth the bother of a curtain. This window has a view out onto a part of the service lane at the back of the building. In the early mornings the black jacks that grow two, three feet high against the wall cast their scraggly shadows across the cobbles. People do not believe they are observed here in the service lane. Some feuds, a furtive sex episode, children playing truant from school. Some of this I see, and I do not interfere. And then, speaking to Hafferjee today, I sense a new movement outside the window. I peer out over his shoulder. Hafferjee turns to watch with me. A man is in the service lane. He has a slight stiffness to his body, as one has who become accustomed to the need to be constantly on his guard. He scuffs against a loose brick by mistake, and then goes back to kick it away. I see that he wears worn-out army supply boots. The man is stringy and tanned so dark he could almost pass for a native. He leans into the metal staircase and begins fiddling with his fly. The long arc of his pee is caught by the wind. They are all over the place now, these ex-servicemen returned from the war, coming back as if the world owes them a living. Coming back, their wild loose eyes unsettled by events we can never know, taking other people's jobs.

Even if Herbert had not been declared medically unfit, I doubted that he would have gone off to fight. He was not that kind of a man. There is something oddly familiar about this tramp in the service lane. Reminds me of one amongst the group of men I saw in the Company Gardens yesterday afternoon. Yes, the very same! For a time the man's frame blends into the shadows so that you can't properly tell whether the shadow you see jutting across the cobbles is a piece of a limb or a piece of darkness, a rafter or weed or tree, blocking out the cast light. His face is half in shadow too. And then from this distance I catch a glimpse of his stubborn morning shadow and pursed pink lips. His eyes are cloudy. Even from this distance there is a glimmer of sunlight behind them. I reach over and touch Hafferjee's knee.

'Hafferjee, look,' I whisper. 'See that man. I think I know him.'

4

Herbert Wakeford is not sure whether or not he has cleaned his teeth. He cleans them again, and then he goes out to sit on the stoep. He watches an Indian mynah bird strutting about after kitchen scraps. After some time the bird scuttles off, the grass settling quiet in its wake. One of the nurses brings Herbert his old burlap bag. He nods a thank-you and she walks away. Her firm behind swings out of sight as she goes indoors, leaving Herbert here in the heat of the stoep. He checks the contents of his bag: a couple of fountain pens, a few old notebooks tied together with string, his anvil, bits of leftover rubber, a length of gut and three big-eyed needles, one still threaded.

Herbert picks up a cut-out sole that is half attached to an upper and he begins to push the needle in through the thick dark rubber and out the other side of the canvas, in and out, in and out. His chorea is stilled when he sews. This is because of the pressure of the rubber and canvas against his fingers. Or is it simply because he is making a pair of shoes for his daughter? Herbert cannot say. He only knows that today he must not get the black rubber marks on his best white shirt. There is something different about this day, isn't there? Herbert's fingertips trace the straight grooves of the rubber resting here between his hands.

You can always tell where Maggie has been by her footprints. Herbert knows this, for we liked to speak of it. The other children wear Bata soft-soled takkies, their patterns make wavy criss-cross lines in the dirt; but the print left by Maggie's shoes has always been straight, as straight as the roads through the Karoo. When Herbert rethreads the needle, his hand trembles, a stiff twig caught on the edge of a waterfall. The nurse is back beside him. She stands so close that he can smell her sex. She is tapping him on the shoulder now, holding out his pills. Herbert has swallowed pills here in Doornfontein for almost twenty years. Year upon year upon year, each day, there is not even a break at Christmas or Easter. Sometimes a new doctor comes and then the next week, or the next, the colour of the pills is different or there are two instead of three, or another shape is added.

'Time for your sweeties,' the nurse says.

There are five pills now mid-morning. Herbert counts them. He opens his mouth. The nurse places the pills one by one on his outstretched tongue. She passes him a glass. Herbert takes gulp after gulp of water. She walks on, rattling her medicine trolley. The nurse has moved on without so much as a 'thank you'. Some nurses are like that, not realising how much harder their job would be if the patients were less compliant. The jagged edges of the white tablets get stuck in the throat sometimes. Herbert knows that this can cause thrush. They don't tell you that, in their lists of side effects on the box. In any case, the nurses prefer you not to see the box. They tell you that by swallowing these chemicals you can be the person you were made to be – not hurting anyone or anything.

For so many years Herbert has believed the words of these doctors and nurses, these people that he does not like or trust. How silent he has become, how law-abiding. This special day, for the first time Herbert wonders why he has lived like this for so long; he wonders if there just may be another way.

One night not so long ago, his mind elsewhere, Herbert had dropped his soup bowl on the floor. Immediately he got down on his hands and knees to daub at the spill with his serviette, picking up the broken china and reaching up to put it in a neat pile on the table. The nurses looked on in silence as his body shook and juddered with its task. Herbert pushes his thick needle in and out of the rubber and the canvas and he wonders if the staff at Doornfontein play with his weakness. He wonders if they amuse themselves by trying to train him as one might a puppy and he knows that they do – he recognises it in their expressions of self-congratulation when they succeed in bending him, but not so much that he breaks. Today, seeing all of this, his heart is sad.

'You must have forgotten your yellow pills at lunchtime, Herbert,' the nurse had complained when the floor was clean. 'Is that why you dropped your bowl?'

It is a long time since Herbert Wakeford has cried.

What will happen if he does not take the pills? Will

they see him walking around with his dowsing rod like Moses in the hospital gardens? Is that what they are afraid of?

'They help you,' the nurses say. 'Would you refuse insulin if you were a diabetic? Would you refuse a splint if it helped a broken bone to heal straight?'

How annoyed the nurse had been when Herbert had sent Maggie to live with Sara Highbury! Jane had pulled her lips into a thin line, taut like a thread, and said that Sara could not be trusted to bring the child up in the fear of the Lord, and that they would have to find a way to get the child back and that Herbert should never do such a foolish thing again.

Herbert pulls his thread in and out the other side until there is no more thread left to sew with. He breaks off the thread and, holding the needle, closes his eyes for just a moment. When he opens them, here in the newly gathered brightness of the light, he notices a dried red riverbed of blood like mud across his fingers and down the palm. Strange how the fingers don't recognise the wet, not the way a face explodes the slightest damp from tears. When Herbert cut the leather with his knife to make the straps, he had not sensed a cut, nor had he felt, soon after, the warm stickiness of blood. Those small capillaries of the fingertips, the blood so soft and thin on the thickened finger's skin, little wonder it seeps across unnoticed. Herbert lifts his hand up to his mouth to moisten the dried blood-stain with his spittle, no other moisture to hand. He wipes off the blood marks, as best he can, on the inner sleeve of his shirt. Oh never mind, he can always walk with his arms at his side and no one need know. And tomorrow, perhaps he will wash this shirt and the stain will disappear.

Disappear? How is it that Maggie's mother, Anna Papenas, has succeeded in disappearing off the plate of the earth? She has never sent so much as a Christmas card. She has vanished just as surely as if she had stepped out into the dark night of a train. No one will tell Herbert what had become of his girlfriend, Anna. Not even these nurses who pretend to honesty in matters of the body. Why is it so easy to speak of some things, whilst others are throttled before they even reach the heart? Even a Christmas card would do. But then Herbert does not exchange Christmas cards with anyone excepting for Sybil. She sends out cards early, right at the beginning of the month. Sybil is one person who would miss him if he was no longer here.

Even though it is many years now since Herbert sent Maggie with Cora and she came to live with me, and although it was Herbert's own doing to send Maggie away, there is still an empty chasm where her presence used to be. No visitors. No envious glances. Nothing to make him stand out from the rest in Doornfontein Hospital. There is nothing like a child to ease the passing of the time. The simple matter of the milestones, the smiling, talking, walking – these punctuate any ordinary life with a sense of accomplishment. Nothing left now to make him special. Just a man with his own member for company. Just a man with an empty shelf where a book could be. Not even a man, a half of a man.

Jane suggested that he might get Maggie back one

day. Jane promised that Maggie could come and live with her. A few nights ago Herbert's body thrashed so violently that he broke the bed with his writhing. And they say that in the morning he came out into the dining room without a thread of clothing on his body. Naked as the day he was born. It was not until he saw the broken bed, and the bruises across his ribs and arms and legs that Herbert realised that he had had an attack of chorea in the night. Jane took him aside and she explained again about his illness. She has never seemed afraid of him as others are. Jane has God on her side. And, of course, the blood of the Lamb will heal us of all our iniquities.

'It was called the dancing disease once,' the nurse told him. 'Because of the way the body moves. As if a person is dancing. But the dancer doesn't hear the same music as the rest of the world.'

He cocked his head to one side awhile, as if to show he was listening out for her tune. And Herbert knew that he was set apart in her eyes and that was miracle enough for him.

Perhaps the nurse was right about Maggie. Perhaps there was still a chance that they could do right by her, bring her here and perhaps even the nurse herself . . . It was not out of the question.

'That family that looked after Maggie was no good,' he told Jane.

Jane said that she could have found someone else, if only Herbert had said so earlier. She said it was wrong of him to let Cora take Maggie away.

'I have known Sara almost all of my life,' he said.

'No,' the nurse said. 'It only felt like it because of

your illness. Sara is not your home and family. You have been here with us longer.'

And so that is why just yesterday Herbert sang to himself as he emptied the slop pail, laughed uproariously playing pool with his friends from Ward 19.

How sweetly they had come together, Herbert and Jane. He would never have dared hope, yet nothing on heaven or earth could have stopped it. This is how it happened. Jane had invited Herbert to her church. He sat beside her on the pew. The organ music stirred the deep root. Made it spread its tentacles strong. In church he danced to the hymns. They didn't mind. It was that kind of a church that had already begun to spring up. There was a deep cut off here between the body and the soul, Herbert recognised it at once and so he felt quite at home.

'There is a thing that links us,' Herbert said to Jane. 'A shared primordial sea.'

He thought, but did not say, that thing is disturbed in me. There is no stilling these movements. But Jane did not seem to mind. No way to make the waters still. 'Give me your hat, Herbert,' Jane said as they sat together that afternoon in the peaceful place between the pine trees at the edge of the hospital gardens. And Jane took the hat and from it she took the stone where Sara had once sewn it, so carefully, in Herbert's cap so long ago. The tides of the ocean wash in and out.

'The river gravel has those stones in it,' Herbert said, the words washing in his spittle, his mouth tick tick clicking.

Jane stroked his hair. He reached for her. He could not believe this reckless act, even as his hand began its dancing daring journey across the landscaped gardens of her body. He watched and listened for Jane's objections, but none came.

After quite a long time she began to shudder.

'That's enough now,' she whispered. 'Is this what it is like to feel your body is out of control? Is this what Huntington's is like?'

They walked a little way together, linking arms. When they came level with the hospital buildings, Herbert peeled off to the side and approached the buildings from the west.

Herbert finishes his row of stitches, the special reinforcing across the toe of the shoe, and then he walks to the edge of the stoep and looks out beyond the hospital gardens. The grasses are quivering now like the start of a chorea and the clouds have laid their small shadows across the veld. No one will begrudge him a walk in the veld, one last walk on this important day. He will miss his lunchtime pills, of course, if he leaves. In any case, they make him feel like throwing up, they make him feel strange, dizzy sometimes, and there is always this smell, this lingering stench as the chemicals pass through the pores of his skin and out the other side.

Herbert puts aside his rubber and canvas and needle, puts them under the chair, careful so as not to leave his things somewhere where someone might sit on a needle later (that has happened before). As he leaves the stoep with his burlap bag under his arm, Herbert nods farewell to the other patients seated there. No one acknowledges his departure. Herbert is no longer surprised by this manner of behaviour, for those who live here seldom greet one another – they walk past another person as if passing a piece of furniture. What would it be like to be regarded in a respectful manner again, just like a human being, whatever that humanity might turn out to be in the end? Herbert clutches his bag close to his body as he walks.

And yes, if I could look at Herbert now, just this one last time, I would. And if he could look at me and if there was a possibility that he could hear me, I would ask him, are you sure, Herbert, that this is really what you want to do? Something like that. Could he answer? His yes was yes and his no was no. He has always been this way. But Herbert does not think of me now. He will not allow himself to remember my gaze.

Once inside his room, Herbert closes the door behind him. He tips the contents of his bag onto his bed. Then he pats his shirt pocket and feels the capsule of his wooden bottle hard against his chest. He presses a little harder with the flat of his palm and feels the remorseless pounding of his heart.

Jake Hangklip has recently moved to the room next door. Herbert can hear him heaving and puffing. Jake does push-ups thrice daily in the small space between his bed and the wall that separates their rooms. Herbert can hear him counting aloud, ninety-nine, a hundred, a hundred and one, and then there is the thud and silence that always follow these exertions. Jake is the kind of man who does what has to be done. Therefore he can be trusted. Herbert takes his small wooden bottle out of his shirt pocket, checks again that the stone is still safely contained within, and then wraps the wooden bottle in a large sheet of paper torn from his notebook. He takes his candle, lights it and carefully seals the edges of the parcel with its dripping wax. Then he repeats this with another piece of paper, and another. Finally, satisfied, he writes out an address and a note, and leaves these in the passage, on the small candle-shelf outside Jake's door.

Herbert Wakeford returns to his room, selects a few things from the treasures strewn across his bed and stuffs them into the pocket of his shirt. Remembering all of this, but forgetting his hat, Herbert steps out into the fierce hollow sunshine.

* * * *

I wonder now if Herbert was dizzy without the pills that day that he left Doornfontein. I wonder if he felt as if he was about to black out, walking out there in the veld. He must have been dizzy, I think, for the brain gets used to a drug, as to a situation, a person for that matter, so that when it is taken away, there is a time of disorientation, a time it seems anything is possible. Would he have known to put his head between his knees, not to remain standing or sitting? Would he have known that it is very important to return the blood to your head where it can keep the brain alive? I know what it is like to have this kind of vertigo – I have been prone to such spells ever since coming to this country; perhaps it is the heat, or something else.

I remember one such occasion a few years back now,

still in Brakpan. The blackness swirled all about me. When it passed over, for a few moments I did not know how long I had been gone. I walked slowly over to the kitchen window holding on to the edge of the table. Supporting myself thus, I looked out into the back yard. The afternoon was bathing everything in its softer golden light. Maggie should have been long returned from school. She had taken to dragging her heels of late. A number of weeks had passed since Frank and Sybil had disagreed about the fate of the young buck eating Sybil's peas, yet we were still reminded that Frank had wasted a loaded gun. Sybil would not let any forget it. She didn't say a word, but that look set in, as if the queen's own face, haughty, the date, the place of this event franked across her cheeks and forehead, cut across that eye. None other but his hand that done it.

Standing at the window, supporting myself against the table's surface, I thought I heard a gentle tremor amongst the fallen leaves. Leaned over the table a little more, then motionless, hardly breathing, peered out. The same young buck, it must have been, emboldened, walking across the grass. Such a gentle thing, and earnest, believing the world owed it a living, much like a child.

'You're lucky that Frank is not home yet.' I said it out loud.

The buck that had been stepping across the expanse of our yard more delicately than any fine lady startled, scampered away.

And what should be coming over the rise of the road then, but a man, Frank himself no less, I could tell from

126

the gait, but his form all taken over by a clutch of billowing orange fabric, locked in embrace, as if a woman of the night. And what he carried there, the torn parachute, though worn in parts, I could see as he came closer, was the most extensive bolt of orange silk I had yet encountered.

He told me later he had found the parachute in a field, no one claiming it, rotting in the hot sun, brought it home.

'Manna from heaven! Manna sent from heaven! Look at this!'

I ran through the passage to their side of the house, out the back door to help. Frank was cursing and spitting from beneath the load and the way it tangled on the knee-high weeds, and caught on a fallen branch, insisting Sybil not waste the silk. She stepped from the open doorway behind me.

Frank always came home at 2 p.m. in such a frame he'd eat a horse, he'd clocked in at 4 a.m. to water down the stopes before the team came in at six. Frank liked to take the early starter shift, found plenty of use for the afternoons, could earn a double wage by fixing cars, or build a house.

The parachute was still wet in patches from the dew despite the sun's heat through the morning. Must have lain out the previous night, and the damp grass beneath and over and amongst all the folds had no opportunity to dry. We spread it out so that the dark wet patches lay open to the sun and air.

Later, before sunset, all three of us and Aloma too came out to fold. An awkward shape it was. Maggie stood on one leg, the instep of her raised foot against her calf, then skipped a little aside and pulled a clutch of fabric against the bare skin of her long dark-brown arm gone so golden in the sun. I noticed again the size of Maggie's feet – so tiny, the shoes Herbert sent her were still too big.

Aloma Maggie smiled as the silky smoothness of the parachute silk rubbed up against her, a look in her dancing eyes I did not know. Sybil would not have the silk cut, not yet. I turned away.

'Come on, I have other work to do. Pull that piece straight out there, Aloma. Come on now.'

But first, before we set to folding, Frank wished to cut the ropes where they were sewn. Pushed his blade with such a force from somewhere close to his body to attack the string that I stepped back a little lest it slip. I feared that knife in his hand, though he meant me no harm at all. The imprint of his boots in muddy patterns stamping out his path a gentle brown across the orange silk. He enlisted us, the closest arms, to help sort through the tangle of ropes. I pulled out the twine and let it run between my fingers. Frank tugged on the other end of the rope's length, winding it neatly all around pieces of cardboard for tares.

'A handy thing to have around the place,' he said. 'Must be best quality twine, Sara, to hold a man in the sky.'

I thought of such a man, drifting down from the heavens like a feather. Wondered where he was now, the one who had flown down, neither bird nor bee.

'We may pass him in the street without knowing him,' I said.

The man out in the service lane is rising now as if preparing to leave. Hafferjee and I watch in silence.

The man moves as someone injured and repaired again, something slightly mechanical about him.

'He's aware of his body's movements,' murmurs Hafferjee.

And then, as quickly as he came, the man is gone. I go closer to the window pane, peer out to get a better look, but he has vanished.

And then I see it. Frank. For a moment I would lay my head on a slab, I feel so sure. Hafferjee just shrugs his shoulders and changes the subject. He is a clever man, Amin Hafferjee, but he doesn't fool me. There is something here he is not telling me.

On the subject of telling and not telling, in my experience, a child reaches a point at about eight or nine, when they need to keep a secret. More than that, the whole child becomes a secret so that you almost don't know whom you are dealing with any more. Maggie became like that when she was staying with me. It happened sooner than I would have expected. Even at only eight years old, she stopped talking to me about the things that mattered to her. It would have been useless for me to tell her that I wished to be a companion on her journey not a spy.

For some years, a parcel would arrive for Maggie from Herbert. He would send Maggie shoes each year for her birthday, each year one size bigger. If given the choice Maggie refused to wear them. She was happy, however, with the stamps, always eager to tear them off, leaving the letter untouched. I am thinking now of one day, the day of the stamps, I call it now. It must have been shortly before I lost her. Lost her? As one might lose a coin? No, it was more simple than that, more completely irreplaceable.

It started out as an ordinary enough day. I was busy with the laundry. Maggie was seated on the floor of our living room soaking envelopes to get the stamps from Herbert's letter, and others that she had been collecting. Her bare crossed legs were dark and strong against the brown-squared linoleum floor. The water became slimy with dissolving glue, and the softened shards of envelope slid away from the stamp. Aloma Maggie helped the separation gently, then laid the stamp face side down on newspaper to dry. Later I saw that those stamps, the Union 2d, pictured a kind of Johannesburg, recognisable as the City of Gold. The picture was ahead of its time, it showed grand multi-storeyed buildings as a backdrop of the kind I have heard they have in New York. A mineshaft in front, with a miner's headgear tossed to one side on the ground. I walked in carrying the whites, the firm corners of the sheets, where the cotton is doubled up for the quarter-inch hems, brushing against my nose. I was only just able to save myself from falling head-long over her long legs, jutting out at the knees. Maggie shifted position to squat on her heels, then folded her legs right under her, resting on her calves. She fell forward over her knees as her eyesight reached to the bowl in front. A flimsy monarch's head floated face side down in the water, half attached to a slip of paper. Her finger pushed it further down to get it thoroughly wet, to loosen the glue.

Because she had entered the age of secrets, Maggie

did not tell me about the stone throwing, the facts of the matter, the Afrikaners against the English, who threw what, even when I saw the rocks in her school satchel, mica, veldspar, all types, some as large as my own hand, and one day, her bleeding mouth. And most importantly, she did not tell me about her teacher. Later that afternoon I was to meet him in person with no warning.

Earlier that day, some black children had come around for some collection; they were upright, shining bright as if someone had polished their cheeks with Brasso rub. Those children did not show the dirt, not like Maggie. Or perhaps, I think now, perhaps they simply had more relatives around to keep them clean. Too often those years, Maggie seemed crumpled and unkempt – her hair unable to fall in a straight part. But it was not Maggie's dishevelled appearance that troubled the school. When the teacher knocked, I had no choice but to open the door. He wore bluish-grey shorts and knee-high socks to match, not a spot of fluff visible, the lines of the socks pulled straight, with a comb tucked neatly between his calf and sock. When he came in, his step was heavy and preoccupied with his own importance, a quality I have seen oft-times in a man, though seldom in a woman. His thick and hairy thighs moved as purposively as pistons.

'Mrs Highbury, madam, Aloma is a child who could be performing better at school; she is an intelligent girl.'

I wondered then if perhaps Maggie had showed some sign of her father's illness there at school. Had Maggie, like Herbert, tried to strike a rock, hoping water would spew out like Moses? Is this what brought the teacher here? His fleshy eyes looked about him, the curtained-off cubicle in the living room, the sewing lying about, our single narrow bed with its crocheted cover visible through the open door to the bedroom.

I gestured towards the chair. 'Please.'

He settled himself in the old car seat that we used as a chair. It was our only easy chair. He did not take the tea I felt I had to offer. The old car seat did perfectly well for us, for Aloma and myself. Yet beneath this man's bulk and the common way he had of moving, I knew it could only be a matter of a moment or two, and something would give. The seat's balance was surely unaccustomed to the weight and movement of a man.

Sure enough, as I feared, the seat gave out a loud creak as he shifted his weight towards us, as his finger wagged in my direction, a spring suddenly popped out of the upholstery with a sharp rip – a sound that I, as a woman of cloth, know all too well. Released from its tight leather prison, the wire from the seat's spring was there in the open air, a sharp exposed innard, sprung free, digging into the teacher's thigh.

Maggie gasped.

The young teacher did not look down, did not appear to hear a message in the fabric ripping. It may as well have been but a dog barking in the distance, or the workings of distant machinery of no relevance to himself. The spring was stuck half into the fat of his leg so that the join was not really visible. It was obscured by the dents it made in his white flesh. The sight of it all made me think of a toy, a jack-in-the-box

132

perhaps, a small tea box, a stuffed sock, a red-spotted kerchief at its neck. Take out more springs, and sell such toys down at the Saturday market in town. What could I get for such a toy?

'She should be performing better,' the teacher growled.

An urgent reasoning sound came into his voice. Something about the papers, Aloma Maggie's papers. I tried hard to listen. A cold, cold breeze blew onto my skin. He was going on and on about the papers. His eyes did not leave my face, so that I had to look away. The coldness of the air at that moment, and the way it moved independent of the wind outside, brought back to me the day I had met Amin Hafferjee and his factory women standing in lines in the fruit processing plant near Paarl. Rows upon rows of women, the air cooled by the huge arms of swirling fans above, their hands moving in unison, the rivers of pears their focus, huge rivers of pears. I felt that cold factory air blowing all about me, but I had no rivers of pears swirling before my eyes, just the teacher's hairy thigh and the weighty foot beneath a leather shoe all shiny under its frail coating of dust.

'Red tape it is, nothing but red tape, these Dutch are full of red tape.' I wanted to say it out loud. But I forced myself to listen; listen carefully now, Sara, to this thick and threatening voice from the fresh-faced teacher once more.

He wagged a finger at me and said something about the papers, Aloma Maggie's papers, and what in fact was the truth about her, and he was aware she was not performing as she should, and I should take care.

'Madam, take care. There is something here that is not quite right.'

And he was wondering if the Social Services should know about this. Maggie must have the papers before the new school term or they would make their own enquiries. He tipped his little brown felt hat at me as he left.

And so that was how it started: for Maggie and me, whether we stayed, or moved north, crossing the Limpopo River to see what lay on the other side, as I had begun to fancy, I would need the papers, proof of Maggie's birth, proof of my right to her.

Maggie stroked with her fingertip the small gold queen's heads on those stamps from England. She wanted me to tell her about that place. Even then, so young, she preferred a squirrel to a meerkat.

'To look ahead is better than to look back,' I told her.

Perhaps somehow I should have found the means to take her somewhere else. I don't know how, but spirited her out of this country, taken a fresh start. And then, in time, the letter arrived. I found it in Maggie's school bag. Frank read it over and agreed with me, the meaning: the headmaster of the school would set the authorities on to me, unless I produced a valid birth certificate for Aloma Margaret Proctor and a letter from her parents giving me the right to care for her. Frank advised that I write to Herbert, request that he urgently send Maggie's papers. I did. I wrote again the next week, and the next and the next. No response. I began to wonder if Herbert still knew how to read.

*

Hafferjee has been busy whilst we have been talking. He has my open newspaper before him, the one in which I was completing the crossword before he arrived. He has not continued with the crossword, but rather set himself the task of filling in the cavity of each letter with ink. The *p*s, the *d*s, the *e*s and the *a*s and of course the *o*s. Has already made his way down an entire column of text. What a thing to choose to do! Reminds me of what Frank later told me, in one of his many letters, about the war. 'Whilst in training in Egypt, some were ordered to dig holes and others to fill them in.'

'The war took me by surprise,' I tell Hafferjee. 'Frank gave in his notice at Daggasfontein Mine, and joined up.'

'Do you want me to go with you? Do you want me to take some leave and go with you, Sara?' Frank not cowered by anyone, not then or ever.

What would the doctors at the hospital think of a man with tattooed snakes slithering across his forearms? Why must a man stamp the softest, the most beautiful of his skin? He had a suit, but no, you would not get Frank to stay in a suit in the summer. And in any case, Frank was to leave for war, as soon as they would have him. Maggie and I would journey to Doornfontein alone. I would wash and press her as if we thought she carried a pedigree in those bloody papers they would not give me.

I had given up the idea of going straight to the officials myself.

'See, the girl is here, is this not proof that she is born? See, this is her name, Aloma Maggie Proctor. Aloma, what is your name? Is this your name? See, this is her name, what else is a person called but by their own name?'

But I was afraid to speak freely, afraid if some official was alerted that this were not my child, he would take her away from me.

Frank was experienced by then, in his mid-forties, but strong, always having led an active life, and they accepted him soon enough. Having worked in the mines he was classified as a demolitions expert, and also worked as a motor mechanic. So he had a good rank and was well paid. We did not know then if we would ever see him again. Then, just before I thought he was due to leave, they turned him away. He was resident for a time in a dormitory of an internment camp called Baviaanspoort. He was kept there for disobeying orders or some misunderstanding over whom and what he was fighting for. Frank stayed there with the Italians, Germans, many of them Nazis. He later told us how they got into their nationalities for football and were all comfortable enough and got along well. After some months, the boredom grew too much for some and many of them, including Frank, were persuaded to fight on the side of England. First Frank went for a three-month spell at a training outfit near Ladysmith. And then at last all was set, he was to go.

In anticipation of leaving for the war, Frank developed a greater fondness for Sybil. Whilst training at Ladysmith, at least each fortnight he took French leave, getting someone else to answer his name at roll-call. Hitched home on a lorry for the weekend.

Most dashing in his uniform, cheeky smile he had. Joked about with the steel helmet and its camouflage net, sticking leaves and twigs as if a genuine bushman, then some white daisies he'd picked from a field.

'Hey, Sara,' he called, setting the daisies waving in the breeze with each bob of his head.

And that is how we photographed him. Despite that, afterwards in the pictures, I saw a seriousness to his face I had not noticed at the time. The eyes were the same, those cloudy eyes not quite hiding the light behind them. He straightened his shoulders and seemed to stretch up from his spine, with Sybil beside him. Yet still you could see how small he was, small and solid as the rock so recently mined below the surface. That hardness of a miner's frame is never lost, however many years he rests.

By the following August, our men were issued with a uniform of loose-cut brown serge that I far preferred, beret to match, strong brown boots that would last some well beyond those years.

The day that he left on the train, Sybil and Maggie and I stood together on the station platform, the men in their uniforms all about. At 11.45 a.m. the carriages laden with soldiers and shouting waving berets disappeared from view. We had all been surprised at the train's departure, on time, so that some were almost left behind, tardy in boarding. We walked back to Plot 481, a weighty silence hanging all about us. Sybil drew in her spittle so as not to dribble, making a spittle-sucking sound. Although I had grown used to this sound from Sybil, had heard it many times before, that afternoon it seemed to shake me as loud as the crack of a fine china plate if I dropped it. That and every sound thick in the heat of my ears. The stones skidded beneath our footsteps across the yard. Frank was safely bound for Durban, and from there would board a ship to Egypt.

Sybil's step did not falter. Without Frank beside us, or there to bark out instructions on his latest project in the house, Sybil seemed stronger, more herself, as if he left behind some solidity, made her sturdier on her own, when he was around he claimed it all for himself. Ah, not much further now into the shade of the house. I did not know it then, but that time was to become a watershed for us – either side, different streams of our lives would flow, maintaining their course, as if they were never joined.

At about mid-afternoon, a sudden violent wind signalled a storm to come. Sybil sat indoors, had begun sewing for Frank already, her mouth stuffed full of pins. I stepped out to bring in the washing from the line. The handkerchiefs and Sybil's old thin orange undergarments slipped from between my fingers and the clothes-pegs, pulled by the wind. My thinly clad arms so recently clammy with sweat, began to chill. I had to kick the door to open it, hardly had time to enter before it slammed hard on my heels. I went over to the kitchen window to look out, wanted to see if that sudden, now again, rattle on the roof was hail or if someone was throwing stones at the house, that was common in those days, by those for and against the war.

A tin drum outside blew over, rolled around

the garden, came to rest indecently toppled. The rubbish, old tins and packets and bits of paper, flew around, the Brakpan sky littered with crying birds, then beaten by the stones, the hail falling from the great height of the heavens. Sybil pulled pins out, and stuffed them back into her mouth, their heads pointing outwards. And only as the rain itself begun bearing down on the iron roof so that our words sounded hollow and muffled inside our heads, Sybil told me, shouting to be heard, that she had no plans to stay here at Plot 481 with Maggie and me. That house I thought of as my own home by then. She would go to stay with her Pops in Durban.

Within a week, Sybil's suitcase lay open on her bed. She was packing a good selection of her plentiful garments, stuffing them in with hardly a space for a stocking left.

'You two'll be all right here on your own?'

Each word dry and mumbled falling from the corners of her lips. I walked over to where she stood hesitating at the doorway.

'Write down the address for me,' I said. 'I will get Frank's letters forwarded.'

'He'll send the letters straight there. Frank has Pops' address. But here.'

She took the pen in her large hand and came over to the table to write.

'Here, in case you need to reach me.'

I watched the big blue square of Sybil's rear end pulled over to one side by the weight of her bulging suitcase disappearing down the dust of the driveway. After she had rounded the corner at the black-painted letter box standing on its pole at the gate, I threw the piece of paper she had left on the table into the grate. Blue flames grew up all around to embrace it.

I have not seen Frank and Sybil since then – three years have passed. It is possible that the war could have changed Frank, made him someone I hardly know. The human body can take on so many forms so that a person can become almost unrecognisable.

I have, for example, a photograph of Herbert, one taken before his illness, those days when the bright globule of his presence seemed to leap from the page. You can almost see the colour of his eyes, despite that the photograph has no colour. Yes, I can remember that blueness now – such a shade – every other pales against it.

Maggie too changed whilst I knew her. There was the need for secrets that I have already mentioned, and there were the natural changes that happen to a child who is letting go her innocence. And then there is the matter of the scar. If it is necessary to apportion blame, I suppose that the scar is my fault, and yet how could I possibly have prevented it? I blame the boy too – he was there visiting when it happened.

He had knocked once and his thin freckled arm was raised to knock again when I surprised him by opening the door.

'Yes, young man. Are you looking for Maggie? Well, she is busy.'

But the boy knew me, and was undeterred. 'Is the

dear Maggie here? I will not stay, thank you, but I came to invite her to play.'

'No,' I said. 'She has work to do.'

His face fell, and Maggie sank down into herself in despair, the light all gone from her eyes. I could not abide it.

'Maggie is not going anywhere, she has work to do. If you behave, you can stay here and help her. You hear that, Maggie? You do not go out of my sight.'

'Yes, Auntie Sar,' she said.

And I knew it was just a recitation of what she thought I wished to hear. What did a child learn in school these days? Yes, Auntie Sar. No, Auntie Sar. Waste of time.

Not a half an hour later those children were racing through the kitchen, Maggie was chasing the boy with a rain spider, holding the hairy creature by one of its fragile legs.

'Maggie. No! How many times have I told you not to run in the kitchen? Can't you see I am cooking here?'

Maggie's hands were raised to swirl above her head. As she turned to answer me she collided with the corner of the kitchen table, her loose elbow flew out, knocking the handle of the pot on the paraffin stove. She shrieked as the boiling stew splashed across her shoulder and chest. The hot oil of the stew soaked right through her dress. The fabric stuck to her skin as if by glue, a second printed skin. Through her tears, she looked for the spider but it had gone. I fetched Maggie her shoes to take her off to the doctor. I always insisted on shoes. A barefoot child is a poor white, I maintained, but a child who is shod is a child from a home of culture and refinement. It is a matter of hygiene as well as decorum. And so I fitted on her shoes, the ones that Herbert had sent last birthday, whilst she whimpered and trembled in her shock. We took a skirt and blouse too, for when the dress was peeled off.

That was a nasty scarring from a boiling stew, red and angry, wounds I dressed every day with powders and ointments as the doctor instructed. After that, I sewed all of Maggie's dresses to have long sleeves to her elbows, and high necklines, the lumpy welt should be covered, kept out of the sun.

I look across at Hafferjee. I do not believe that he knows anything about the beauty of a real human scar. He is not like Frank: 133 bones broken underground and still counting.

'Does Maggie still have that scar?' asks Hafferjee.

It is as if he can read my mind. I look at him as if he too has lost his marbles.

'Why, if she does, however much she changes, you can always pick her out,' he says. 'A person with a scar can never be lost in the crowd.'

I am thinking now of how one morning some months after that accident, Maggie had come out in an old blouse she had found that had no sleeves, open too at the neck. I startled, but not at the scar slung across her left shoulder creeping out through the armhole, opaque white and twisted against her thin tanned skin. I was taken aback that she should so expose it. Put it out for all to see. Maggie wore her delicate pink blouse that day with an embroidered daisy chain around the neck's opening, but even that was not sufficiently strong to pull the eye away. I recall now how I felt in myself an urge to stretch out a fingertip to touch that thickened tissue, so unnaturally raised above the rest. Recoiling all the same for its strangeness to me, so linked to a pain long forgotten now but still recorded here faithfully in the body's make-up, brittle and caked in the sun. The sweat pores must be all blocked, I thought, covered over, and yet still the twisted ropes of the skin, here and there rising to the surface, shone with the brilliance of oil. This seemed out of place in Brakpan, where all the roads are hung about with signs, the landscape gone unnoticed. None any longer there recalled the way a rock too could be made beautiful by the weather, and a tree-trunk twisted with time into a form that Herbert had once loved, walked miles to see. Something not right about this, Maggie exposing her shoulder to a public viewing, stirring up base emotions in a passer-by. Someone who just wished to mind their own business, get on with life, form a greeting, faced with this evidence of another's experience so forged and beaten. This evidence of a sorrow which cannot be unborn. Surely it is only proper to keep such things to yourself? Did Maggie know it disturbed me so? Is that why, soon after, she had changed her clothes?

'No. I don't think Maggie still has that scar,' I say to Hafferjee. 'I expect it is all healed over by now. And if it isn't, she should keep it covered.'

*

143

'Hafferjee, I think that was Frank, the man I have been telling you about, Frank and Sybil. I think it was him out there in the service lane.'

Hafferjee does not answer me. I do not think that Hafferjee and Frank would care much for one another if they were to meet. You could not find two people more different if you went looking for them.

5

The fierce heat of the late-morning sunshine goes straight through Herbert's bare head and wakes up his brain. He breathes deeply. Each breath injects further determination into his gait. He covers the ground surprisingly quickly for one so unused to walking. His arms are a little out to the side, marching a little, the head jerking as if on a spring, his eyes bouncing up and down in his skull. With the body moving, Herbert's mind is stilled for a moment. His body propels him on and on. The shadows shrink to almost nothing in the noontime sun and then come out again the other side. It is so hot out here, hot and dry.

As he walks, Herbert imagines himself back at the diggings in Bloemhof. It feels as if he is almost there, though in his mind, he knows things must have changed. The piles of gravel would be all worked over for a start, so that not one remained, the earth would be flat, the holes filled in, levelled out, as if that time had never happened. The shanty, corrugated-iron houses are most probably razed to the ground, yet the place would still be familiar to him – perhaps the way the sun hangs at a certain place above the horizon this time of day. Yes, he must be getting closer to the diggings, he is sure to be walking in the right direction, he can sense it. The Orange River flows more slowly, right through the town further on. The river must have been dammed higher up.

Herbert believes that he is accountable for what his body does. What is it to be good? There is a pain that links his shoulder and head with such a thread or rope that he is in no doubt that they are connected. He walks across the raw bright plate of the earth and keeps going, hoping to walk right in to a cool cleft of a mountain where a stream is just flowing. Somewhere north. Keep walking to soak up the sun and keep on walking to find refuge from it. A small patch of shade cast by a lone pepper boom is a lake to him. But when he comes closer, its low thorny branches make it impossible to get close to the small pool of respite cast by its foliage. The earth soaks up his fate within her decomposing leaves.

When Herbert comes to the small stream, he walks up it a little, just in case someone will try to follow his tracks. His canvas shoes are sodden with mud. At last he is in sight of the junction of the railway line. This is the place Herbert knows, a place he has long dreamed about. This junction is where the goods train slows down for its rise up the northern contour of Vrou se Koppie. Herbert sees how granite is harder than flesh, more durable. He falls, picks himself up, and a few paces on he falls again. Each time he gets up, he pats his pocket to check that his treasures are there where he put them. His fountain pen, notebook, a picture of Maggie, a biscuit wrapped in a handkerchief, a roll of Triple X mints.

Almost every rock and boulder seems intent on tripping him up. He must hurry now. He hears the train coming from the west, hears it and then it comes into view.

Just in time Herbert reaches the little copse of gum trees growing in the dip, green from the run-off from the slope. The train sends out her deep whistle, the one he has heard from the hospital, the one he has listened to, like some new bird or beast, some lowing cow, for so many years. The train is almost at her slowest point as the weight of its carriages slow her ascent. Herbert stumbles onto the place where the line rises again just beyond the gum trees. The first car is just passing now, belching out its steam and coal emissions, black sense-filling clouds. The fumes puff around his sunken cheeks in a kiss of welcome. These link him for a moment to the engine's power, invite him to share in it. Car after car passes, the long slow train travelling south. The last car is in sight now. With the weight of the goods and the incline of the line, the train is slowed to almost a halt. The ladder at the side of the car stretches up, straight up. And at the top of the car it curves up elegantly against the blueness of the sky and out of sight. Herbert teeters forward. He stretches out his hands and feet, puts the ball of his foot across the hard cold bar at the bottom of the ladder and holds onto the rung level with his shoulder and begins to climb. It is easy, one foot in front of the other. It is peaceful here, up above the world looking down.

I can always step back down the ladder's rungs, he thinks. But when he tries, the train is already moving far too fast and his homeland is disappearing from view. So Herbert gives a sort of a wave. The back of his hand flaps up and down like a letter box on the hinge of his wrist. He will hold on here to the topmost rung, love this feeling of the hard metal against the bones of his arms and at the balls of his feet, hold on longer until the black cloud blows across the sun, and keep on holding.

Somewhere around Fourteen Streams Station the goods train gives a little jerk as it passes a crossing and Herbert Wakeford falls from the ladder. He falls on his side and rolls down a rocky patch of earth. Herbert falls asleep for a while there where he lands, just a little way from the railway line. He sleeps deeply, that unnatural sleep that brings dreams more real than your own flesh and blood.

There are dead fish scattered on the riverbanks after the river floods. And then in his dream, Herbert comes to a sort of a hotel. This is a new place with a frontage identical to the Queens in Springs. Inside, there are cigarette stubs in the ashtray. A woman stands beside him.

'There is still a chance to find the stones the old people missed,' she says.

A boy is riding a rusty tricycle around a veranda, his bare limbs stained with its red polish. Herbert stops for a while to talk to him. He shows the boy some tricks with elastic bands making patterns between his fingers.

When he wakes it is almost nightfall. His hands are white with blisters from holding onto the train. You would have thought that Herbert's palms would have retained their toughness from those days of pushing his wheelchair. But no, he has new trophies to show. A marvellous thing, the human body. He is bruised too, where the ladder bumped against his thighs. Herbert appreciates these things and he laughs. He watches the dusk falling and then the sky growing bright and deep with stars. You can almost dip your hand into the darkness and pull them down. He recalls Maggie, and how, aged three or four, she had asked him for the golden coin of the moon.

'The moon, Herbert. I want it. But I want it. I want it.'

Her tone had been more and more insistent and if she disbelieved anything, it was only Herbert's assertion that he could not just stretch his arm out of the window and pull it down for her. Soon after, she had gone to live with Sara. His shoulders are pulled tight and stiff now and he can feel a large puffy bruise spreading across his cheek and closing up his right eye. He takes half of the biscuit stored in his pocket and eats it. Then he curls up into himself for warmth and tries to sleep here on this rock, this smooth granite boulder that for a few hours longer will retain some heat from the sun.

When the moon is at its highest point and the rock has grown cold, Herbert is still awake. The light comes and he finds a stick and combs his hair. At last the sky is fully bright. Herbert leopard-crawls up a rocky granite outcrop and looks out across the countryside. From the way the vegetation shifts, and the direction of the road and the line, he judges that this place must be some twenty miles from Warrenton. He has come out for a walk, has he not? Herbert chooses a lucky direction and steps down. And so it is that he pivots his legs, one before the other, through the ant-washed dirt. He tries to forget that he has become a man who is afraid of falling. A suddenly vertical ground squirrel looks at Herbert then just as suddenly flattens itself to run off. White darting butterflies swoop in and out amongst the white-tipped grasses, these grasses that are already green in the stalks because of the summer rain. Perhaps if he makes it as far as Vryburg he will be free. Herbert cackles to himself at the thought. His laughter sounds small and empty in this vast landscape and he feels ashamed.

After a time the railway track comes over a rise. From afar he sees the place where the line is traversed by a road etched into the landscape, as if someone had taken a blade, and seared it right through a piece of old dusty leather. Gouged out to the horizon, the long swathe of it.

'We all get to the same place in the end,' he says, to no one in particular.

He walks on. Vultures circle overhead, brown and beautiful in their feathered forms against the strong blue sky.

'We all come here, whether by foot, or train, wagon, or wing or any other means,' Herbert says.

He looks down. The silent line does not answer or applaud. When Herbert reaches the junction with the road, he looks at its hard gravel and imagines the trials of the journey had he been walking on that gravel and not clinging on the side of the goods train. He turns away from the line and steps into the road. He does not sing. For almost a mile the northern border of the road is edged by short sticks to stop the restios from growing into it. And then he comes to a section where there are fences either side. Beyond these sit a patch or two of dead trees with new shootings from the centre. Herbert marvels at the twisted beauty of the bare-limbed trunks and the mobs of tangled sticks.

There must have been a fire here not so long ago. He is not so far from a settlement here, not so far. A fire like this would not have started on its own. He turns off the road, out into the open veld, he walks in the spaces between the vegetation.

It is only later that day, when the shadows have begun to lengthen, two, three feet across the scrub, that Herbert feels himself collapsing. He lowers himself gently to the ground, trying but not quite managing to avoid the red mounds of the anthills. He braces himself against the biting of the ants.

'What about Maggie?' Hafferjee's voice cuts into my thoughts. 'Does Maggie think of Herbert as her father?'

'I can tell you what happened, Hafferjee. I cannot tell you what is in the mind of another, or what should be.'

But this does not seem to answer Hafferjee. He tries another tack.

'Did Maggie enjoy the visits to see Herbert at Doornfontein?'

I have been wondering of late if anyone from the hospital will be attending Herbert's funeral. The funeral is to be on Saturday. Hafferjee, I presume, has come here today to ask me about the arrangements. I am certain his visit is Cora Rynhardt's doing – her gossip travels faster than a telegram. I have heard nothing from Jane, neither do I wish to, even Cora is afraid of her. Jane has Maggie in her grasp and there is nothing I can do about it. You cannot fight a person like her. She occupies a nether world and does not broker reason. The only thing I am convinced of is that Maggie, the way I brought her up, will see through it in the end. She will be free one day. And so I tell Hafferjee what happened the day that I took Maggie to Doornfontein to see her father. Have three years already passed since then? Where have I been? I feel I will go mad like Herbert if I do not allow myself to tell it. And so I tell him how we went to try to get the papers, proof of Maggie's birth. The school was on to us to provide them, and Herbert had not answered my letters, not one.

Around lunchtime, the schools closing for the holidays, I began to pack a few items. We would leave on the 6 p.m. train. And we would return with Maggie's papers. I would take them to show the teacher at the start of the term, but I would not let the school keep them. The little brown suitcase lay open on the bed, I started with socks. Perhaps that was my mistake, perhaps if I had started with something else . . . Aloma walked in from school. She needed to rest, to calm herself, and have some of the stew I had cooked for our lunch. Instead, she took an apple from the bowl on the side table, and began to eat it as a chimpanzee might, glancing across at the suitcase. What would this child turn out to be? Between bites, and talking with her mouth full, I suddenly heard through the spittle what she was saying.

'I am not coming.' She swallowed and said it louder. 'I am not coming to Doornfontein Hospital. I will stay here.'

'You will come with me, Aloma.'

'I will not. I shan't.'

'You will.'

I continued packing our little brown suitcase. I did not look up lest she weaken me with her gaze.

The priest's voice billowing against the half-empty pews in the church of St Peter's, Sunderland, his words becoming stronger, not softer over the years: Honour your father and mother so that your days may belong upon the earth, he had said. The Bible snapped closed before him, with its thin gold-edged pages that could be so easily torn. Oh. I held firm. If the child would destroy herself, I would have no part in it.

'You will come, Aloma. You will. There is no discussion here, no argument. You will do as I say.'

'I shan't,' she said. 'You lie about him, you say he is sick, he is not. He is in Doornfontein, and that is because he is . . .' And she tapped the side of her head with a bent finger. 'You lie about him, to me, to Sir at school, to the headmaster, to the shop lady, to Johannes, to everyone. You are a liar. I hate you.' And as Aloma Maggie spoke, her face grew unaccountably plump with shame. Whatever I had said to Maggie about Herbert it was only to make her life easier.

'He is your father, Aloma. You owe your life to him.'

The afternoon light fell in a hot square through the bedroom window disregarding the flimsy curtains drawn in together against its rays. Aloma Maggie looked quietened now and I rolled a pink towel and pressed it in the suitcase, beside her cardigan. I began to wonder even as I spoke, of course I could not be sure of Herbert's role in the whole affair. And as for her mother, of this matter we did not speak. And against that, a clean blue skirt, pressed blouse, spare undergarments, a book and

153

pencils with which she may draw during the long journey, a pack of cards for Patience. And her flannel nightgown, yellow and brown and white with floral print, I had matched the pattern at the seams and the join was hardly noticeable.

But just as I thought I had won this battle and that Maggie would be compliant, her face clouded over and she turned. She threw the thread of her apple core into the corner of the room, an action she knew would irk me further. Then she put out her arm, strong as a snake, and with a swipe or two she begun to undo my careful work in packing. I took her hand away with my own, and she flinched, speaking through the crumple of her face.

'If you try to take me,' she squealed, 'I will run away. I will go to live with Cora in the Cape, I shall, she will take me on picnics to the beach.'

Something in me delighted in her resistance, even as I hated it. It lit a flame in my fatigue and desperation that once ignited seemed unable or unwilling to be quenched.

'You will come with me, Aloma,' my voice raised to match her own. 'You will, if I have to drug you. I will take you there, and leave you there, I will leave you at the madhouse with your aunties if you do not listen to me.'

And I felt my heart outside my body's carcass pounding against the sun-warmed rocks outside. From this I knew that I was shrieking at the girl. Whilst my anger horrified me, I did not rein it in. I felt an inkling of cleansing, cleansed of what I did not know, for I had tried my utmost to do right by this child. Yet nothing I did was ever sufficient, was ever good enough. I could not give her what she needed, and yes, she needed too much, the child's insatiable appetites were what angered me, her sense that she knew what was best for her, when she had not yet lived. That would destroy us all. This seemed my duty and my calling, to control her. Aloma's dark sad eyes began to fill silently with ink, waiting for me, the quill, the pointed brush.

I moved her hands away from their interference with my efforts. I must get the suitcase repacked. We could still easily make the 6 p.m. train. Then I saw again her eyes that were overspilling with darkness.

'Maggie, no,' I cried. 'No, no.'

But she had already aborted my embrace, was off barefoot down the street, throwing marbles with Johannes, barefoot scum of a child. I hated her for making me thus.

But I did not choose you, I whispered to myself as I folded her nightdress once more into its corner. Fate wheeled you to me that day at the station.

I had to insist on this, and insist I did. Aloma eventually relented, agreed to come with me, but only when I promised her that, on the way to the train, I would take her to a restaurant recently opened in Springs. I said she could have whatever she liked on the menu. Could choose and order herself. They offered sweets of many kinds, ice-cream with coloured syrups and the most enormous fruit salads you have ever seen, covered about with swirls of whipped cream, encasing strawberries especially brought up from the Cape.

The next day Maggie and I sat together on the tall restaurant bar stools, seeing our reflection in the shop window, looking out. Aloma Maggie's pixie face turned suspicious on me, her every swallow of green ice-cream cemented my guilt, thrust another bolt across the door. Once I had provided the child with some relief, once she had wanted my love, had nourished herself alive to me.

'Go away,' she cried. 'Be gone. You do not understand me.'

And I did not, but I made no claim to understanding. The girl and I shared a bed, was this not sufficient? Nothing in the world, it seemed, would ever pluck this living spear from its hole in my side. Yet she was still the child and I the adult. I had to do this, to take the child to see her father, for it was written that way. Not one of the Ten Commandments? I could not be sure, and possessed no Bible. Thou shalt not kill, thou shalt not commit adultery. Honour thy father and mother. Yes, I felt sure this had been once engraved in stone.

'But didn't Moses throw the tablets down the cliff so that they broke?' Maggie had once asked me. 'And didn't he strike a rock with a dowsing rod and make water come out, just like our Herbert in the hospital gardens?'

I did not have all the facts of the matter to hand.

'The good Lord will have to take me as he finds me,' I said. 'Whether I am wearing a crucifix or not. And in this here house, young lady, we shall honour the Ten Commandments, we shall. When the good Lord gives you your own personal tablets of stone, you tell me what these are, but in the meantime we shall abide by these ten.'

As we left the restaurant, Maggie insisted on pushing the bar stools back straight under the jutting-out counter, and she wanted to take the tall and fancy glasses to the

156

hidden kitchen to wash, but I said she could not. I paid the bill we could scarce afford, despising myself for my weakness.

I tried to speak again about these things on the train, as we journeyed at last to Doornfontein.

'Sar,' she said. 'Auntie Sar.' And she took my hand. I could feel my face hanging with fatigue.

'Let's go together,' she said excitedly. 'And put our heads out of the window to feel the wind.'

So we did. We stepped out into the passageway and pushed open the door to the snaking metal floor that linked the carriage and the dining car. I pulled the window down a good twelve inches, as far as it would go. Aloma's long plait was instantly whisked out of the window by the air rushing by. The girl had grown her black hair long in an untidy tail behind her shoulder. I stood beside her, and pushed my head too out of the window. As the train passed through a cutting and began to pull up the incline, clouds of steam pulsed from the engine's wheels and the whistle sounded long and hard. In the face of the wind, I loosened my pins, shook out my long hair, thin and greying. It swirled around my face and throat like a blinding cloud. The wind was acid with ash and sulphur so that my eyes stung with pleasure. My scalp felt free and light, as if a child again. The cool air of the evening surprised me, right down to my skin's exposure, the wind ripped up my shirt's shelter, and slapped it back against my skin to stick there flesh to flesh. I heard myself suddenly laughing, a soft laugh that came from a deep place, like a hum. I looked at Aloma to share with her something of my exhilaration, but she was already replaiting her braid, pulling back from the window, away from me. Was that when I began to doubt myself? Was that when the seeds were planted, that would later result in my being prepared to let her go?

In any case, that day I leaned further out into the wind, so that my shoulders were right out in the cold, and as I did, I caught sight of the new moon rising. I felt compelled to howl and bay, knowing that the rushing air would sweep my song clean against the wheels of the train. And so I cried out, louder and louder. It was as if my power pushed the very train through the night. After some time I felt fatigued from standing, my back beginning to ache, and so returned to our compartment to rest. Maggie was nowhere to be seen. Within the hour she returned, flopped into the seat beside me, and wanted to know what I had packed for our tea.

Maggie and I arrived at Doornfontein at around 8 a.m. The line, its sheep field and bend of poplars marking the last homestead, had changed, a new settlement grown over, and so our arrival surprised me. We had to scurry to gather our bags and be out before the train whistled its departure. We entered the hospital grounds on foot. Vast spaces, enormous buildings that seemed still deserted, waiting patiently for a disaster.

Whoever designed this place must have been expecting a public outbreak of madness. Like the Spanish flu of 1919, they will be wheeling us by the barrowload to Doornfontein; our hearts still beating, however, and spittle drooling out of the corners of our mouths. The papers will be here to report it.

I looked over at Aloma, who marched on, a few paces away. As I slowed, so did she, as I speeded up, so did she. I focused on stopping the twitching that had begun at the corners of my lips. Maggie had not rejected me entirely. The girl and I were still linked by an invisible thread. My hand slapped at the small weight of the buzzing horsefly setting onto my leg and our footsteps crunched across the grass scythed down into stiff clumps, most as high as one to two bricks. Perhaps as high as three in this greener strip over here – the faster growth of the grass after its cutting must be a sign of a water-course or a stream flowing underground.

I had once told Maggie that there was magic in nature. This I believed. And if you stood on a single thick clump of grass long enough with both your feet firmly planted, perhaps the energy of the grasses growing focused in that concentrated clump would grow you taller. For some months we had gone out together to the edge of the veld beyond the road in Sallies Village to stand like this. I had not grown an inch. Maggie stood clutching out at my arm as she lost her balance, the bright purple and red stars dancing behind our eyelids in the midday heat. The memory stung, for I saw that the child had suddenly outgrown me. Walking across the scythed grasses towards the hospital buildings I clamped shut the instinct to speak of those occasions. What else could I give her now? When I opened my mouth to speak it was not the real child I had in view, but an old picture I caught myself about to address, and I stopped myself just in time. More and more I did not say anything to her, just let her be, this girl-person foreign to me. Sure enough, when I glanced over at Aloma, her face set in seriousness, she hardly seemed to notice the magic that had once set her jumping in excitement.

'Please, Sar, Auntie Sar, let's go and stand on the grasses. I know it is working. See how tall I have become today.'

But that day as we approached Doornfontein Hospital, her eyes looked straight ahead, vacant with a distant gaze that did not see what was right before her eyes. She did not have a glance to spare in my direction. We came closer to the building, to where the grass was shorter still, almost a lawn it formed here, but soon gave way to patches of foot-barrened earth amongst the hospital buildings. A wide door stood ahead of us now, with a brass knocker that had been painted silent. The green paint on the wood was peeling in places. I sank into my body as we stood at the door. Not proud of the bright colours of my clothes. Shoulders hunched over, like a rotten apple, soft in the centre.

Sometime before I had left the Cape, Hafferjee and I had fallen against a door like this, although that day a strong wind had blown up my skirt. Climbed three weary church steps after a violent rustle of leaves in a graveyard, my shoulder fallen against the door in fatigue or dissolution. The next day I noticed I had been bruised, my large thigh puckering purply-brown on the side where it had fallen against the ground. The colour of old wind-fallen leaves, as if the ground must leave its stain no matter that the next day, in the post office queue, bringing in the laundry, it were as if the thing had never happened. Squatting in my mind like a dream. I had walked into a post, into furniture, I could not remember, it was a bad day, I was not myself. Does Hafferjee remember it now? Of course he must. He gives nothing away.

*

I lifted my hand to push the door. It would not budge. I tried again, twisting the handle and pushing my weight against its resistance. Then knocked and called.

'Ahoy, Ahoy. Dry land ahead.'

There was no answer.

'Come, Maggie,' I said. 'Let's try the other side.'

As we stepped down, a Hadedah Ibis came into view, its bad eyes looking for beetles, and its long legs crab-like walking around the weedy flowerbeds. We skirted around the bird, and hugging the building, approached it from the rear. A side door was ajar, and we stepped into a dark corridor. There were doors leading off to either side that may open at the flutter of a hand, but as we came level with them, I saw that their hinges were so dusty and cobwebbed they must have been closed for centuries. A lone form in a gaping faded blue dressing gown that still did not tell me if it be man or woman suddenly scuttled from one side of the corridor to the other. I thought perhaps a man and a woman should be dressed in blue or pink to tell the difference. I should suggest it. But the apparition had gone from view before I could call out in greeting.

It was then that a loud and confident voice sounded behind us.

'Maggie. Maggie. It is Aloma Maggie. How lovely to see you here, girl. And such a big Maggie you have become. I hardly recognised you.'

I turned around to see who this was, and Maggie stepped back into the shadows, but the voice was upon her, embracing her.

'Come out into the light, child; let me see you, child, there there.'

As she and Maggie moved towards the window, I was delighted to see that this was the voice of authority that had found us, a nurse's uniform, epaulettes bristling on her shoulders.

I did not know how this nurse recognised Maggie after so many years had passed; it must have been that Herbert showed around the photographs of Maggie that Frank sent each year with Sybil's Christmas card. Frank liked to tease Herbert with the pictures, as if Herbert did not have trouble enough with confusion already. In the developing Frank liked to put Maggie's head on someone else's body, or make a twin of her, identical, facing inwards like a mirror. Perhaps we would not have to see Herbert after all. Perhaps this nurse could help us in our task. Perhaps she would be sympathetic regarding Maggie's papers, perhaps they were even here with her, or she could pick up the telephone and make the arrangements, as this type of person is wont to do, to get them posted immediately. But that was not to be. No, the nurse bustled ahead of us, then she vanished as inexplicably as she had arrived.

We waited for Herbert Wakeford in the Visitors' Room at Doornfontein, Maggie beside me holding my hand. We stood in order to distinguish ourselves, for we were not at home here. A few patients on straight-backed chairs were scattered about the landscape of the room like pods fallen from a tree. Some blown now and again by a wind, but most stationary, staring into space, that one winding some elastic thread onto a tare, she was most casual in dressing gown and slippers of a colour no longer clear. She sat upright like the others. Never forgotten, invisible books balanced on their heads.

'All know some training in posture,' I said to Maggie, forcing myself not to whisper.

One or two of the patients watched us with open faces but not a single one greeted us or made an introduction. Then from the dark square of passage behind the door, Herbert walked in. He saw us before we saw him. He was making straight for us, was almost upon us before I realised it indeed was him.

That day it was Herbert's shoes that early on pushed themselves into my gaze, my eyes embraced Herbert, though uncertainly, starting from his feet of clay. I searched each crack, each line, as if the soft canvas and rubber soles held a clue, a warning that I should take note of, gain a chance to garner some strength by an early knowing. Yet Herbert's shoes that had known him all these years were as soft and lovely with age as they had always been. The first change I saw at Doornfontein Hospital was not in his shoes but his ankles. I had not recalled his ankles like this, stiff and white, the stalks of his legs artificial flowers planted in the soft real soil of his shoes. As Herbert stood before us, he seemed to have a confidence here in this institution that he had not had on his visits to Cora and I in the Cape so long ago, a confidence he had not had even before his injury. This Herbert I did not know. My eyes lifted slowly the length of his legs beneath their trousers. He had always stuttered about – that was our Herbert – even when motionless he seemed to be moving, trembling. Now his pose was pretending a confidence, a stability – that was the first whiff I had of the sin of it. Herbert had once said to me that this hospital was his home and family.

'I want to go back, Sara; please take me home,' he had said.

This I had come to accept.

'Sara . . .' Herbert continued to speak, as if we were in the midst of a conversation, which I swear we were not.

'Sara. I know this may be hard for you to hear, but I must tell you.'

He began speaking with no greeting, just like that. After a six-year silence, only shoes each year for Maggie's birthday without so much as a note or drawing to accompany them, shoes she did not wish to wear, only wore because I forced her. Because I schooled her to honour her father, having no mother that I could rightly place.

'Sara, Jane has told me that I must tell you.' Herbert's mouth full of words mixed in with spittle, rattling against one another as the wave pulled back to sea.

Then he hesitated a little, a glance thrown in our direction for the first time. He was looking right at me, his eyes not marbles but stones, pebbles they were, looking at me, heavy, dark and skipping.

'Hello, Herbert,' I said. 'This here is your daughter, Aloma.'

He did not remark at how she had grown up, how beautiful she was (and she was a most attractive child in the dresses I made her), neither did he stoop at all to offer an embrace as another father might. And as we stood there, I could not help but notice, through the gap between his shirt buttons, for he was still man enough to refuse to be clad in a dressing gown in daylight hours, I could not but help notice, for the pale skin of Herbert's chest had only known a few fine hairs before, I could not help but notice, how it had grown thick and dark, a carpet it was now. He stood in front of us. Maggie said not a word.

'Maggie, greet your father, child,' I wished to say to her. 'Say hello, ask how he is today.'

Herbert still held the strange smell that he had had the time he came and visited us in the Cape. Only worse. Something acrid or burnt seemed to come from his flesh.

'Sara . . .' He was still speaking.

And each time he spoke I looked up, expecting a miracle that would return him to some semblance of his former self, but it did not occur.

'Sar, I am to be let out. I leave here. I am certain I will leave.'

'What? When? Where will you live?'

For the moment that he said it, I realised that I did not want the man to live with me. It was best after all that he was a resident here in the hospital

That is how we had found him. He believed he was on the cusp of his release, that this was the day they would let him out for good. No one would try to catch him and bring him back. But they never had, you know, they had never tried to bring him back.

I saw that day at Doornfontein how Herbert Wakeford was something combed, something shaken through so that everything precious and uncut and potentially sharp, everything had been robbed from him whilst he lay helpless on his bed there, whilst he walked through the hospital gardens, his thin pale-blue cotton dressing gown hanging from the cliffs of his shoulders, without any fear. Yes, this was evident to me, even before he opened his mouth. Ahem, ahem. His flesh spoke to me of slackness. Something about this was not quite right. Something was perverse to me. I did not want to know of it, to speak of it, to hear any more of it, but I had to hear the end, I had to continue, the two of us in this game, I was trying still to fit the broken pieces together in my mind.

'I am to be married, Sar,' Herbert said.

I had thought, nay, not exactly thought, but expected, that Herbert would age as I had known him. Whether in this institution or not, I thought he would age in keeping with how he had lived when he was alive to me. I only saw this had been my belief when it was not fulfilled. When this unspeakable, unimagined happened. I bear witness that Herbert became another. I had only myself to blame. I had held to my beliefs, as a sleeping child, long since passed over into the other realm, may still clutch a stuffed animal or toy, a mother's finger. This is what has happened then.

Standing there, I could not help but recall a night, any of those nights, huddled around that Chinese woman's pot-bellied stove for nothing more than a cheap drink and some conversation, Herbert sipping his water as if the Lord's own blood, my sides sore from laughing, his slow gentle smile beside me, a smile that did not demand anything, it just was, and how it had made me soft. Is it too much to ask that there be some thread of connection between the years?

I had expected Herbert to age as a chameleon. For this is how he had lived, elusive, silent, wild. Startling across a sun-warmed stone, then lying still and focused, beady eyes staring, his body the hard still centre of the world, everywhere wavering about him. A vein perhaps visible as pulsating skin, the only evidence of weakness, his snaked tongue lashing out at passing youth, the dense scrub of his hair turning grey beneath my fingertips, his colours more pale now in light and shade, but just the same. I had expected that he would age like this. And this was the totality of the first surprise of my visit. He did not age in this fashion. And then even before my eyes, beneath his ill-fitting thin stripes of trousers, his member, not properly contained, unfurled towards me like a sail filling with wind. But this particular ship was without rudder, and what good is a sail in the wind, when the vessel is shot through with holes, is sinking before we have even lost sight of the land? Seeing him then, my heart was a bolt of lead, weighing that inter-action heavily. While the sight and smell of Herbert stirred in me no desire, only a kind of repulsion at the memory of desire, I could see even then he was a man. I supposed some woman could use that fact, had used it. I thought of this, and then I recalled what had happened. Surely I had known. It was the nurse's doing. This is what that nurse wished to gain from our Herbert.

'I am to be married, Sar,' Herbert had said.

And he said it over and over in my head. I heard him say it. I did.

What sort of a woman could wish to marry a man like that? My knees trembled at the thought of it, the sin of it, like the jelly she would make him for his tea. A man who has lost his threads. There is a woman in the world, a nurse nonetheless, who wishes, nay intends, nay who is betrothed to humble Herbert himself, a man whose mind is shot through with holes. Cannot remember what he had for breakfast, cannot remember whether he had made love, cannot remember the past, our past, our memories, our love. Those, once drained from him, were drained from us both, from this time on, could not be replaced, grown cold to me, though I had not wished to let them go.

'And, Sara, one more thing,' Herbert said. 'I don't know how to thank you for your help with Aloma, whilst I was kept here in the hospital. But Jane says it will be only right for her to come now and live with us. When you are ready, I will come and fetch her myself. She is fond of Aloma.'

'It was the nurse's doing!' Hafferjee alighted on his first insight of the morning. 'That nurse put the school up to it. Their problem with wanting the birth certificate was just an excuse, a way for the nurse to get Maggie back.'

'Perhaps you are right for once, Hafferjee,' I say. 'Perhaps you are right.'

Before we left, Herbert came out to show Maggie and me his suit. It was too short for him. His ankles stuck out, a badly cut charity suit in synthetic fabric. Herbert in a suit, the knobbed bones of his wrists and ankles showing. Even so, you could tell from the thin strip of brighter fabric that the trouser and sleeve hems had been let down.

Herbert's hands were cold when he took mine to say goodbye. Hard and cold, they broke off my heart. And as I took Maggie's hand to lead her away, the nurse emerged again. It was as if she had been watching us all along, and waiting for her moment to spring. I was not so shaken up that I didn't notice. I saw her through the window from the inside as we marched down the corridor. She was out in the yard, positioned to have a view of our exit, standing in the shadow of the building on the patches of dust worn through by many feet. When she heard our approach, the nurse threw down a cigarette from her mouth, twisting the butt with the hard heel of her shoe against the ground. As she swung towards us to intercept Maggie at the door, the imprint of her heel drifted out one last silent cry of smoke.

Aloma had been weeping, but swallowed it. She clutched a parcel to her chest. It was too large for the child to carry, but she refused to let me touch it. And as we left, the nurse pushed a further gift onto Aloma. It was a life-size picture of a red rose, a photograph that had been touched up in full colour, dew drops glistening, more real and beautiful and pure than any rose could hope to be.

'For you,' she said. Aloma looked at me uncertainly.

'For you; yes, take it, take it home,' the nurse said. 'It is yours to keep.'

Aloma said nothing, but clutched the rose against the parcel, with her free hand.

And so we had left without the papers, just this useless parcel and a picture of a rose. They would be fetching Aloma Margaret soon enough, Herbert had said, there was no need for any papers.

On the way back on the train from Doornfontein to Brakpan, I did my best to cheer Maggie, I thought to tell her a tale. I had to shout to be heard against the noise of the train, loud with its rattling wheels and shooting steam, now and then the canvas slapping the carriage sides where they were open to the wind, for that day our seats were in the third class.

'Once upon a time, a long time ago, there was a young girl . . .'

I did not know the story, how it would begin or end, but I opened my mouth just the same. Maggie seemed already to have forgotten, her face wet with tears. Her body wriggled with expectation and the sun itself shone through her eyes. And so I continued.

'Once upon a time, there was a young girl. The girl was nine years old,' I exclaimed in excitement. 'Like you, she was no good at sums, but like you had a fine hand in writing.'

My voice was hoarse from the wind that snatched my words from me, but I persisted. The carriage shook as it turned a steep corner into a glade, and for a moment Aloma's face was hidden in the shadow. When we came out into the sun again she said nothing, but she looked away, out at the flying grasses and scrub bush of the Highveld. We would soon be approaching Springs, the white dust mountains of the dumps coming into view, in the west, Crown Mines, then after we crossed the city, the start of Sallies. She looked down into the tracks screaming beneath the weight of the train and I don't know what she saw.

'Maggie.' I said it loudly, but leaned my body right over hers and cupped my hand around her ear so that the two men opposite slumped into their overalls would not see my speech.

'Maggie, listen, this is important. I have kept back one stone from the diggings.'

Maggie's eyes lit up, for she knew that the stones carried the wealth of the world.

'Feel it here,' I said.

And I pressed the hem of her coat into her hand.

'Take care of this. You will always be free.'

In my heart, it was then that I began to let Aloma Maggie Proctor return from whence she came. It was Herbert who had done this. This was the day I began to let her go.

The fact that it was not really a stone, the fact that what lay heavy in Aloma's hem was simply a piece of cut glass, red as wine, that I had pulled off a wire bracelet found in the hospital gardens while Aloma was in the toilet, and had sewed it in haste when I sent her to search for a glass of water at the dining car that was right at the front of the train, that did not bother me. Who is to say the true value of this gem?

'Perhaps it is a real fancy stone in truth,' I said to myself.

It would make Aloma feel better, and this was its purpose. If she ever wished to sell it, as I had tried to sell a stone one day in Cape Town, she may be disappointed, but that was not my worry then. I had done my best to put a light in her eyes, and that was all that mattered.

Yet when we arrived home I saw that it was not the stone, but the picture the nurse gave, that Maggie loved. To this day that picture lies wilting in Maggie's stamp album, stuck down with glue.

A little later that night I felt Maggie's warm body slip out of the bed beside me. Soon after I heard her busy unwrapping Herbert's parcel, a belated gift for her birthday. I don't think that Herbert even knew his daughter's age. She showed me the next day. I could see that she did not like it. It was a hat, knitted it himself, Herbert said in his note. The hat was red, as red as the shale in the Cape, the colour that perfectly matched the coat I had sewn. I don't know how Herbert would have known about the coat before our arrival, but here he had matched it with a hat. He had an uncanny sense of things that man. All stuffed about with newspaper to make a bigger parcel.

'An unnatural sort of a thing,' I said to Maggie later, 'for a man to have learned to knit.'

I have to admit that it had crossed my mind even then that if Maggie grew up to be unpredictable and difficult like her father, if she inherited Herbert's illness and had to be fed soft foods like a baby, forgetting how to swallow, surely it was better that she was out of my house? Who amongst you would be my judge? Who amongst you would willingly live with a person who has lost their marbles?

Following one's simplest desires oft-times brings short-lived relief. And so that night, when Maggie eventually hid her parcel and its wrapping, and crept into bed beside me, when she was surely fallen like a tree, I untangled my body from her crumpled limbs, and pushed my way though to the living room where I knelt and placed my forehead on the worn patch of the carpet where the warp of the threads was exposed.

The faded oranges, reds and blues of the carpet's pattern swirled in and out at the edges of my vision. My hands lay just within a square of cold white moonlight with criss-cross patterns from the window's panes. As I considered it, it became apparent to me that it was not the events of that visit to Doornfontein, but rather my expectations of the events, now so thoroughly disappointed, that tormented me most intensely. To have expected a resident of Doornfontein Hospital to act in a sensible way, this was my folly, and how could I, Sara Highbury, have been so foolish? When it comes to untangling the muddle of one's thoughts, no one else can help; none can help unravel the knots and wind those thoughts patiently onto tares, the mind is a private place, you may as well just accept it. I had never before been afraid of the dark but I did not care much for it that night. I longed for the warmth of the sun on my skin. When I could bear the darkness no longer I reached for a box of matches in the dresser drawer but the matches broke off one by one as I tried to light them. I could not even strike a match so that the wind would not blow it out. I tossed the box not yet empty towards the dustbin, heard it land softly on the heap of fabric slivers from last week's cutting, did not save the flint strips.

Cats creep about at night. Undercover a cat can be a nasty sort of a creature I had not so long ago been reminded.

Before Maggie and I had left Doornfontein, walking across the clumps of grasses to the road, our path had taken us upon a cat playing with a bird so thoroughly frightened that only one thing must be certain to her, that the future was certain, and that it would end like this anytime now, in torment. But still the bird continued the game of trying to get away. Why did the bird not just give up and die? Did she continue for the sake of the cat? I did not know, and at times I myself would wish for death, but it did not come when I wished for it. As we had come level with the two of them, the cat pulled its prey away to be half-obscured beyond a scraggly hedge-bush, then, watching us, waited motionless, the bird trapped beneath its paw, until we passed. But glancing back a few moments on, I saw the cat had already resumed its game with, if it could be, an even greater vindictiveness than before.

As the stronger light came in at the window, I noted how all the pounding of my fists on the floor had not left a single imprint on the carpet, its pile so thin and worn that nothing showed. I nestled my forehead again into the dusty carpet, roughened my forehead so that I could feel it red, the pain anchored me, held me here, stopped me from trying to fly away. My hands were clenched into balls of dough, hard and old.

At last the small birds began a soft calling in the trees. Then the ibis who nested south of us, on the island in Brakpan dam, flew over the house with their loud morning cries. Their broken-voiced wailing often surprised me, how soon the dawn was coming, but that long night it was not soon enough. I would prefer not to dwell on that day, the day she left, so I circle around it with my words, like vultures. Not like the ibis – the ibis fly in a straight line.

They took Maggie away. It was left to Herbert now to take his brush to the wide-open ink pools of her eyes,

174

and there was nothing I could do about it. There is still nothing to be done. I have never felt so helpless. Jane is like that. You cannot cross her.

'Where did she go?' asks Hafferjee.

And so I tell Amin Hafferjee that the child Aloma Margaret Proctor had gone with Jane. Herbert willed it. And after that Maggie came to visit only once. She filled the room with stories of the caterpillar she saw, the spider that surely must be poisonous for it had a body as fat and round as a match head, the discarded moth wings fixed to the window, the dogs that sat at the corner fish shop hoping for scraps, and every Friday, for Jane was Catholic, the fillet of fish carried home wrapped in newspaper. Of her school and friends she did not speak. Yet I know that for a child that age, the friends are usually the most significant.

'Perhaps she works as a servant in Jane's house, that is what I think,' I say to Hafferjee. 'Perhaps she keeps Maggie there to be a servant to her, to cook and clean. On the other hand, Jane seemed to want her, that's what Herbert said. Perhaps Jane loves her as I do. Now that she is older.'

Hafferjee snorts, as if a horse tetchy with a fly.

'What is love?' he snorts. 'Define it.'

'Do not curse the Holy Ghost, Hafferjee; do not question God himself.'

'Is Maggie still there now? With Herbert gone, what does this mean for the child and her new home?'

I have not heard from Maggie since that first visit some months ago now and therefore I cannot answer him. Silly, but Maggie's silence towards me feels like my failure. One of those unpleasant secrets about yourself you do not want others to know about.

Soon Hafferjee will go and I will be alone here in this place, with only the residents for company. Strange how the most unlikely of people can bring comfort in one's time of need. I want Hafferjee to leave now. I feel so tired.

The ex-soldier that we had watched a little earlier today through the window is back now. He sits on a loose brick in the service lane, looking left and right over his shoulder as if checking that no one is coming. I trace the pattern of his movements in my mind, testing against my memories, trying to find a match. He seems to be writing something in the dust with the toe of his brown army boot. Hafferjee coughs, one of those forced little coughs he has, to remind me that he is here sitting across from me. I look up and see that his eyes have seen the same as mine. Hafferjee smiles at me, that half-wry shy smile I know so well. His smile stretches out the rosy swelling of his lips.

6

When Herbert wakes the next morning his soft underbelly is covered with reddish welts where the ants found him. It does not concern him that his body has formed swollen red ridges at the site of the bites. He takes these as evidence of being more firmly stitched now into the soil that he loves. None can wrest him away, not any more, this is his home. He is lying close to a reddish-black watery stained rock. The rock is covered with lichen in parts, like an ancient seascape relic. A golden armadillo lizard startles across his line of sight. It stops motionless, secure perhaps in the knowledge of its armoured tail. Is it Herbert's imagining that creature's stomach with its blackish pattern seems rounded, harbouring young? Unlike other kinds of lizards, this creature bears them live, no eggs.

'I am unable to catch you,' Herbert apologises, half-aloud.

He is thinking to himself of the roasted feasts he enjoyed whilst growing up near the mines on the Reef, and his father catching prey like this. His father too knew the earth, until he, like Herbert after him, lost control of his body, was helpless against the storms of chorea. Not having had the benefit of an institution like Doornfontein Hospital, Herbert's father had succumbed quickly to his illness. He had begun to stumble, lose his balance, his temper, and then died, somewhere out there, alone. It was best that the old man died alone, Herbert thought. Better to be alone than with those who do not understand. And was it all as swift as Herbert recalls it? Or is it just the kindness of memory now that has compressed each day of Herbert's childhood into a minute, the years into a lightning flash? Flies come with the warm odours of the day, drawn to the moisture on Herbert's lips. He lets them drink. The blister on his bottom lip feels spongy against the hardness of his teeth.

When Herbert looks up again, the lizard is still watching him. Herbert is sufficiently hungry. He stretches out a hand but before he can complete his swipe, the lizard has rolled into a ball and disappeared. Herbert looks at his empty palm. This reminds him of the rest of the biscuit in his pocket and he eats it. He has no sooner licked the last crumbs from his fingers than he thinks that he hears a voice.

'You will get caught in the storm out here, old man,' someone says.

Herbert lifts his hand to shade his eyes. He watches but as no silhouette appears against the sky, after a time he sinks back into himself.

'Old man,' says the apparition, half-wavering above him, 'what are you doing here?'

The small unruly fish of Herbert's thoughts scramble to get away. He spits it out.

'Herbert Wakeford,' he says. He is proud of himself, how after all that he has been through, how neatly he is able to thrust out his hand, neat and firm, like the unfurling of a member before sex. No one reaches out to take his hand. He is still alone.

It begins to rain. Herbert puts his hand back beneath his coat. Cold needles of rain touch the skin of his face that was so recently warmed by the sun. The lichen-stained rock turns into a dark rapid. How quickly life changes! When the sun comes out after the short cloud-burst, Herbert is lying completely within the shadow of a cloud. Wet through, he starts to shake. There is no one here to take a coat to Herbert, from a dry bag that such a person may have on her back. There is no one to peel off his wet clothes, the white shirt, the suit trousers with darker strip showing where the hem was let down. There is no one to offer him a glass of water and there is no one to be glad with him that the sun may yet warm his back before nightfall. There is no one to wrap a coat around him, no one to pick him up, light as a bundle of quivering sticks, and carry him home. He lies alone and his long legs jut out at the knees in sharp angles like a shaft station. He looks longingly at the sun falling on the higher slope. He lies there just missing the arc of the sun and feeling the darkness fall on him, drifting in and out of consciousness. There is only the rock alongside him and the still air of the world.

On the second afternoon, a vibration startles him. He looks up and sees the slight twitch of a desert crab. Suddenly there are dozens of them peppering the sand, their carapaces red as they are black. They are all turned the same way towards the setting sun. Then, as if at the order of Herbert's chesty cough, in unison each steps sideways and falls, each into its own hole. Only the dimples in the sand remain. Herbert has an urge to crush the sand around the holes, to see if they are linked beneath the earth. Is that underground a place where carapaces touch, or not? He will never know for sure. But then again, who does? Who amongst us, whether a doctor or lawyer, or any sort of an educated person, knows what sort of a world lies beneath the surface? And this is how Herbert comes and goes in his mind. On the third day, remembering about the crabs, he realises what he has to do. He sits up a little, feels around in his pockets for his notebook and fountain pen and he begins to write. He writes carefully, scratch by scratch.

The next day, just the shell of Herbert is left there, half-propped up against a rock.

*   *   *   *

Amin Hafferjee is, I think, encouraged by that small smile we shared. I am not surprised to see him reaching for the leather satchel that has sat beneath his chair all this time. I knew that he came here today with something to tell me. He carefully unbuckles the brass clasp of the satchel and pulls out an old manila envelope.

'A piece of history. Cora Rynhardt gave this to me yesterday.' Hafferjee's eyes are dark ink pools.

I take the envelope. The fish moths have laced a part pattern in one corner and it looks as if the mice have chewed through the bottom third. Although the letter is addressed to me, it has already been opened. It appears that something so old can just be opened by anyone, no respect necessary, like a tomb.

I unfold the letter, an officious-looking document bearing a letterhead and a date stamp in the corner. I notice only the year, 1930. Frank used to say that bad news always comes in a letter. And whilst Cora did not want me troubled in my time of mourning, Hafferjee had no such reservations.

The envelope had been lying at Frank and Sybil's for the past fifteen years, lost somewhere under piles of Sybil's old sewing. Frank came across it when they were clearing out after he came back from the war. Brought it down with him, showed it to Cora, who passed it on to Amin Hafferjee. Seems that everyone else has read my letter already. I hold it out a little towards the light coming in from the window; my eyes have begun to trouble me of late.

The Superintendent
Salt River Clinic
48 Hope Street
CAPE TOWN
REPUBLIC OF SOUTH AFRICA

14 November 1930
To: Miss S. Highbury
Stand 221
Bloemhof

Dear Miss Highbury
NOTICE OF STERILISATION PERFORMED ON MR HERBERT WAKEFORD 13 November 1930
This notice serves to inform you that the above-mentioned white unmarried male, aged 46, occupation diamond digger, underwent a vasectomy procedure in this clinic. The date of the procedure was 13 November 1930.

The operation was voluntary, performed on request by the patient, as he explained that he suffers from a hereditary condition and further, is not in sound mind, and unsuitable for the duties and responsibilities of a parent.

In Accordance with Regulation 14 Gazette 29 of the Union of South Africa, it is advised that wherever possible the spouse/common-law/etc., be informed of the decision since it affects both parties.

I wish you every success in your future happiness.

Yours faithfully
CLINIC MANAGER

A fancy signature at the bottom of the letter is perfectly strung out along the dotted lines. This strong ink is well practised, as if that person had nothing else to do all day but sign his name.

I have never been very good at arithmetic, cannot do the workings in my head. Still, even I can tell it – after 1930 Herbert was unable to father a child. Maggie was born in 1933. He was not Aloma Maggie's father, never was. I look again at the address on the envelope. This letter must have arrived at Bloemhof after I left to come down here to open my sweatshop in the Cape, then forwarded by Kimberley Post Office to Frank. Herbert used to use their address, for they were our first neighbours when we lived there in Brakpan.

'Yes, perhaps that was your Frank out there in the service lane,' Hafferjee says. 'He is in Cape Town – must be – gave Cora the letter with his own hands, she said.'

*

My heart begins a louder beating in my chest. Wherever Aloma Maggie may be, the illness that Herbert had cannot touch her. Perhaps her future would be bright, bright as the sun's rays I had once sewn onto the cover of her stamp album, a gift for her eighth birthday. Why was it that Anna Papenas thought to leave her babe at the mercy of Herbert? Did she know no other man? What of Maggie's father? So who was it then who left Anna with child, and all alone? So many unanswerables. I can describe but I cannot explain. And then I begin to see it – why it is that Hafferjee is sitting here in my office in the boarding house. And why it is that he says that I have not changed a bit. He is afraid of me. I can still send him away just as I had that day in Pauline Kraemer's house so long ago, tell him I never want to set eyes on his little form again. Instead, I hold Hafferjee with the hard stones of my fingers, tightly on the slope of his shoulder, I pull him close to me and speak in just a whisper, lest any of the residents are hovering in the hall. 'Tell me the truth.'

Hafferjee pulls away and leans his bones back against the doorframe as if he will sink right through it. He closes his eyes and turns his head to the side. This time I am not distracted by those long lashes casting their delicate shadows across his cheeks.

When you know a person, when you were once molten together beneath the sewing machines, then you know the meaning of moments such as these. You know what to look for. I whisper those three words close in his ear, 'It was you.'

I watch the unbidden gesture that lifts the leftmost corner of his mouth and sinks away. Is that a memory of the body's cells? A selfish glimmer of Anna's soft flesh reducing beneath his own? The sting of this new knowledge surprises me. I cannot pretend it is otherwise. Something in the human heart wants to be the only one.

'So you just take a woman where and when you find her, Hafferjee? Not even an animal does it like that.'

I think of the photograph Hafferjee showed me – Hafferjee and his two boys and their mother, smiling into the camera each one. Cast in stone – become an object there in the photograph, an object to be cast aside at whim. Hafferjee never pretended to be anything other than this kind of a man.

Just yesterday a package arrived at the boarding house. It was addressed to me, nothing typed, just written in Herbert's frightened scrawl, a letter from the dead. He had had it sent priority mail, despite the cost. As soon as I opened it, I knew that Herbert had not married Jane as intended. Wherever it was that Herbert was headed for after sealing up that parcel, I knew that it was to a place where no doctor or nurse would reach him. It looked as if Herbert had used pages of his notebook for the wrapping, each page carefully folded and sealed with the dripping wax of the last candle that he was ever to light. After I unwrapped the first, I found another page, and then another, and finally, when all the paper was unwrapped, there sat Herbert's small wooden bottle between my fingertips.

I noticed for the first time yesterday the initials carved along its side, it was as if I had never seen that bottle before: H.P.W. Of course – Herbert Proctor Wakeford. Had Herbert been trying to trick the gods, trying to escape the curse of the sins of the fathers that are visited down for four generations, trying to spare the child by giving her his middle name?

I unscrewed the lid. One stone was sitting there. A fancy it was, pink, perhaps a fifty carat. Large stones always come in twos, Herbert had said so, but there was only one stone in the bottle. And he had died alone and indigent, in the veld somewhere. Still, he had sent this stone to me straight from the place beside his heart.

I tipped the stone into the palm of my hand. Held one close to my knuckle as if a diamond ring, then slipped them both into a half-empty matchbox. I am tempted to take out the stone and show it to Hafferjee now, I am so proud of it and I want to tell him how gentle Herbert was, gentle inside himself, despite his troubles.

The day long ago that Herbert came out from Doornfontein Hospital to tell me he had a girlfriend and that they were expecting a child, yes, my mind had been clouded over with other matters that day. Perhaps Herbert had told me something else that day, and perhaps above the sound of the wheels of the train and the canvas as it slapped against the sides of the carriage, perhaps I had not heard.

Specks of golden fairy dust in slow motion swirl in the stream of afternoon light from where the curtain gapes, the dust itself the only evidence of the light's passage. I know from the way that Amin Hafferjee is shifting from side to side, that he will soon be off and walking away from me down the street. Some crumbs of ash from last night's fire blow in beneath the curtain towards my foot.

'Where is Anna now?' I ask him.

'I haven't seen her.' Hafferjee shakes his head.

'You haven't seen Anna, but do you know where she is?'

'I expect she will be all right. She's that kind of girl.'

'You know nothing of what kind of girl Anna is.' I find that I am shrieking. 'You stupid man, look how you have driven your root into every garden and look where it has left you. Look where it has left all of us.'

'Sara,' Hafferjee says. 'That child you loved was mine. Does she look at all like me?'

Our half-drunk teacups sit curdling their milk on top of my desk.

Hafferjee has put his head in his hands. He has wrapped his thick fingers around the ball of his skull as if at any moment he will rip off his head and throw it away.

I have a recent photograph of Maggie. It was amongst Herbert's possessions, given to me yesterday in that old burlap bag. And so I reach for the bag from its resting place behind my desk. I had not noticed before how the clear stretch of fabric of the centre is blackened by a large ink-stain spreading out along the warp.

When Herbert died, he was peaceful, that is what they said. There was no chorea, no choking. I had asked the policeman who gave me the bag if Herbert had choked to death. I always knew, I said, that he would. He had to be so careful of the foods he ate. The policeman said that he did not know how Herbert died, but did it matter now? Something had to help him off the plate of the earth.

He told me that the body was already decomposing when they found him and that we were lucky that there was space on the night train, and as a result the body was already here, at the Salt River morgue, transport free of charge courtesy of the police service, and the body still sealed up in a plastic bag because of the smell.

I push my hands into that old burlap bag searching for the photograph of Maggie. Here a broken piece of an African style knob-kerrie walking stick, carved at the handle, a zigzag pattern burnt into its length. I can feel the weight of it, that Herbert made it. Ah, his old cap! I pull this out and show it to Hafferjee. He turns it over in his hand. Had Herbert clean forgot the weight of the stone once sewn into its lining? A small tear in the fabric where that stone had been, and a few little pinprick hole marks where I had once done the sewing. Stitches long since succumbed to the water's currents in washing, weakened by the heat of the sun. But still my fingers move back and forth where the stitches used to be, wondering if these little holes that remain are visible only to me or if Hafferjee sees them too. Have I already told Hafferjee about the stones that Herbert left me? I cannot recall it now. No matter. Here is the envelope containing Herbert's will. A paper written in Herbert's startled hand. In it, he said that his own shoes soled by his own hand with old cycle tyres were to be given to Sybil, for they shared a special lucky coincidence in the size of their feet. Yet, despite that request, there had been no shoes in the canvas bag of Herbert's belongings. I had thought that perhaps that policeman had stolen them and tried to squeeze his ugly foot in those soft shoes. So I had gone to see the body that same evening, despite that the police had not advised it and I checked beneath the sheet. The cold stalks of Herbert's feet were still shod. So I had Herbert's shoes pulled off the body to fulfil his last request. I can picture Sybil standing at attention, clutching those smelly shoes to her breast, a brown stain against the turquoise blue of her cardigan. Here is a picture. Not this one. This is Jane. She is walking down a cobbled street, shopping bags in either hand, weighing her down, her wild eyes look ready to fly her away, if only they had wings. And here is the locket I had once given Maggie. Did Jane refuse to let her keep it? I had put a picture of myself, five years younger, perhaps not yet fully grey, in the heart. This was after Frank had got his first camera, and took pictures of us. One especially he took for me, my face just the right size to give to Maggie in the locket.

'Come on, Sara. Here in front of the dahlias.'

Frank, not content with taking the pictures, had to set up a darkroom in the house, do the developing, play tricks with the light, put heads on bodies that did not match. We were rich and laughing those days, flowers bending heavy heads, and the house brick, plastered, painted green, in the background. We could not have foretold the way it would dissipate as vapour rising in the heat.

At last I find the small photograph that I have been looking for. Herbert and Maggie are posed together on a bench in the hospital gardens. You can see from the angle of their necks that they are straining apart. Herbert's mouth is hanging open and a small drop of spittle dangles from his chin.

'He found it hard to swallow,' I say.

188

Sometimes you see families like that – however much they try they just do not fit together – it is no use pretending otherwise.

I pass the picture to Hafferjee just as he had long ago passed a picture across to me, that picture of Hafferjee, a white carnation pinned to his tunic top. Hot smelly tears begin to bubble up from the centre of me like a sulphur spring. I am surprised to see Hafferjee crying too. The two of us leaky containers seem to hold all the weeping in the world.

[illegible]

7

When Herbert died, he was peaceful. I know this to be
the case. He could not have choked to death for he had
nothing left out there in the veld to eat, or, for that matter,
to drink. The notebook has fallen to the ground beside
the corpse, I am sure of it. And Herbert's pen remains
balanced across the webbing of his hand so that when
the sun shines on it, the ink leaks out and stains his
marble skin.

You don't dread having a disease like Herbert had.
It just springs on you, unannounced. I for one have
never dreaded waking up one day to find I were the
queen, or some sort of royalty (and Herbert did, let
me tell you; woke up one day and thought he was the
King of France, gabbled away in some strange tongue).
People must know their place. Not many of us are born
to be royal, or rich, or owners of factories or mines.
Many die underground, but not many have Herbert's
condition. I don't care what the doctors say, unlike the
sheep and cattle, the branding we humans wear is
invisible.

On Friday morning, the day after Amin Hafferjee's
visit, Cora Rynhardt arrived. She gave me no choice in

the matter – said she was coming to help me with the preparations for Herbert's funeral.

Cora is balanced on the steps holding the brass knocker, gathering the courage to knock. She teeters there on her high-heeled shoes, a new plastic raincoat is buttoned over her dress. After the usual greetings, we will walk together to the dining room. The smell of mutton bredie, so beloved by the residents, lingers against the walls.

I show her to the small table in the corner.

'We will sit here,' I say. 'There is space to talk and supper is not until 6 p.m.'

Cora has grown a sprinkling of freckles. They are spattered lightly across the backs of her hands like salt, slightly dissolved at the edges.

Herbert had wished to be cremated, had said it in his will, but I would have him buried.

'I will not have flames melt him. Let him feed the ground he loved.' I shook a purple bag of coins, waved it in front of the undertaker's nose when he tried to object.

Cora pulls her shoulder up to her ear. The tears rise up in the dams of her eyes, spilling softly over their walls. There is something about her sorrow that I don't understand. Cora asks to see my hymn book. There are a few missing pages, but plenty here to choose from.

'Here. Choose him a hymn, Cora.'

'"Onward Christian Soldiers". He used to sing it day and night.'

'Was that Jane a member of the Salvation Army

Corps? Did she get Herbert all decked out with medals and trumpets to hurry on the Lord's return?'

'No, Sara. Herbert attended the Salvation Army soup kitchen, there at the bus terminus. He had a square meal every Friday night at the soup kitchen when he visited here in the Cape.'

'Good to hear he was well fed,' I say.

Was Cora envious of Herbert having gone? Has she, despite all the money her father left her, had enough of this world? This is not the Cora I knew, the one who is able to keep up a constant twitter as if a sparrow in a tree.

'"Onward Christian Soldiers" it shall be.'

I write it down to give to the organist.

At last Cora spits it out. Anna Papenas made her promise a silence that she had no right to insist on – now with Herbert gone, there is no need to keep it. Cora tells me more about Anna. I suppose it had to come out.

To Anna, Hafferjee did not deserve the goodness, the rightness of the apples and pears that surrounded him there in the factory. Anna did not know Hafferjee as I knew him. That girl, that fragile bundle of bones that bore his child, she saw the suffocating smock of him, she saw his rigid clocking in and out of that factory like some kind of a machine, not a man, like Herbert. Anna did not admire what I did in Hafferjee – that he worked his way up from errand boy to quality controller at H.D. Jones Fruit Processing. No, Anna saw Hafferjee as a man without courage. She did not wish for someone like that to be the father of her child. Cora pushes her glasses up to the bridge of her nose as she speaks.

'He will take what he likes from this woman, what he likes from another, a bit here, a bit there. He does not embrace the wholeness of a person or thing, just a piece.' That is what Anna told Cora, that is what she believed about him. Hafferjee had walked into a place that was not made for him, as if he owned it. That place in a child that is made open for the spirits, for the wind. But Hafferjee thought that it was his – that was his mistake. So Anna set Herbert up as the father of her child, knowing that in the end the baby would come to me. She did this and then she stepped out into the dark night of a train.

Cora holds out the note to show me. Not having been party to a suicide note before, I could not tell you if these were the usual things that were said in such correspondence. I let Cora collapse against me, holding back my dislike of her smell of old urine and mouldy cabbage.

Mr Silverstein arrives with the distraction of tea and biscuits. It does not escape my notice that Silverstein has decorated the tray with a small upright daisy in a jar.

Between sips of her tea, Cora weeps again and when she has dried her eyes, we choose a stone from the catalogue and write out the engraving.

The next morning, I am up early for the funeral.

I am seated in the very front pew in the small chapel. It is really just a room, beside the caretaker's office. I suppose we must already have sung the hymn that

193

Cora chose. I suppose there must have been a reading and a prayer. The priest who is standing right in front of me closes his prayer book and the sinews on the front of his wrists leap out, that cluster of little roots exposed along a river's cutting. Someone puts a hot hand on my shoulder. It is time now to walk out into the brightness of the sun.

Frank and Sybil are headed this way, he looks as shrivelled and shrunken as a peach stone and just as brittle, just like the man in the service lane. Today he is not wearing his brown army boots but his smart black shoes, the ones that match his only suit. With Sybil leading the way, Frank seems stronger, less ready to be blown away and unlike the man I saw before, his eyes are fixed straight ahead, are looking at me, as he approaches. I fear that I will push Frank over with the weight of my embrace, but he is surprisingly strong, and it is I who has to catch my step. Sybil comes too close, so that I am ill with the smell of her crimplene blue dress.

And then the hearse pulls up, bringing the coffin to the graveside. We especially asked for this, having no pall-bearers of our own. At the sound of the engine, Frank turns to look. He seems to straighten up, grow an inch taller as he moves towards the vehicle. Before it has come to a complete halt, he is already there, his head beneath the bonnet, pulling on leads and wires.

'Grease stains on his best suit,' Sybil mutters. 'I, for one, will not be cleaning it.'

She looks at me, daring me to contradict her.

The engine flinches, falls into silence, only to start up

again louder than before. Frank does not appear alarmed, he trusts mechanics, does not think the motor will leap out and rush him down as I do. We do not wear black. Hardly any of us.

'Cannot keep a black dress there in the wardrobe for the occasion of a funeral, would bring bad luck.' Sybil's voice drops off at the corners of the words as she says it.

Hafferjee is suddenly here alongside me. He feels so close that it is hard to believe that he did not know Herbert, he seems able to share my grief. We stand together staring at the hole of the earth, red earth with dark brown mud streaks. This kind of earth is good for the kiln, but hard on the gravediggers' backs. At the neighbouring stand, they are digging already for the next of us to pass over to the other side. Their arms raised in unison, the hole to be six by eight by three. Those two natives with hardly a piece of intact clothing between them shoulder their spades as we approach and silently disappear. Discreet they are. They will be back soon enough, well trained to respect the right of the family to a time of privacy.

The morning's vapours rise from the sun's heat. Our little group is carefully balanced listening to the priest, half leaning on one another, a hand of cards held upright by some kind of gravity, against our will. I do not know what made that priest so convinced the Pearly Gates would be opening for our Herbert. Suspect it has something to do with a desire to be popular with the living, for who would employ a priest who confessed to doubting?

The sun's warmth begins to weight me through my coat, as if a large tamed cat or child, across my shoulders. I long for some words of truth to be spoken to make this day stand out as respectful to us and to Herbert. Frank is drawing something in the mud with the heel of his shoe. It is remarkable that he does not injure his ankle. And there during the priest's long-winded assertions, Sybil tells me in whispers that Maggie has been found living in a kind of a home near Beaufort West run by nuns. Sybil, unafraid of anything, received this information from staff at Doornfontein Hospital. I take the paper she hands me, push it for safekeeping in the front of my dress.

The priest makes the final pronouncement of rising again and he closes his book.

And then a moan and a thud behind make me turn my head. Cora is crippled down from chest to groin. Silent sobs, muffled as if she had no oxygen, only breathing cotton wool, unable to speak, her body shaking back and forth. Mr Silverstein has come along from the boarding house for the outing: he tries to hold her.

'Leave her, Silverstein,' I say. I move over and pull him away. 'Do her good to have a little cry.'

Nothing one can do about tears like that, let the carpet, the floor, the soil halt their flow. Do not get in the way. The storm will blow over. Like a boy I knew once as a child who had fits now and then, the falling sickness, and after he came around would remember nothing of what had happened. Just knew by the bruised or half-broken nose. A marvellous thing, the human brain.

Cora rises to her feet soon enough, as I knew she would. Her tears quelled, she looks straight ahead through her misted glasses. Her arm brushes against Silverstein's as they come closer to the coffin. The wooden box is soon covered by the brown earth drops as they rain down into a flood.

Our little group is reluctant to disperse. Sybil comes up to me again – she shows me another piece of paper, addressed not to me, but 'To Whom it May Concern'. On it, Frank has written his promise to purchase the hearse, named a price, signed his name.

'Lovely engines, Sara.' Frank joins us, nodding. 'A week to do an overhaul, then we will go north. I've been looking for the right vehicle for some time, lovely V8 engine this car,' he says.

I smile and return the paper. This is the Frank I know, he knows no sacred cows.

'Visit the Zimbabwe Ruins, Victoria Falls. Ever been to an asbestos mine?'

I shake my head, dumb as the day I was born.

'You can always tell a bod from the asbestos mines, the back of his hands are covered by red pimples. Man, asbestos mines are horrible.'

Hafferjee and I, and the rest of us, stand listening, pleased to hear Frank speak, the old Frank, despite his appearance, he is just the same. I don't know if anyone else sees it as I do – how close we came to losing him – it was just a finger's rub away.

'Asbestos comes in fibres, a good one can be maybe a foot long. You can peel the fibres, smaller and smaller, until they are nothing, you can hardly see them. The fibres get under your skin. They are too small to pull out and the body forms these red pimples. A kind of reaction, you might say.'

Frank holds the back of his hand up to the light. The dappled shade covers a thousand itching pimples, dribbling a transparent fluid here and there, like little pinprick injections lost to the air all around. Listening to Frank, his adult baptism in this physical world, it is as if he does not know shame or ever will. Shame, guilt and regret, these words are not words Frank tarries over – whatever he may have done or failed to do in the war. Of what use are these emotions to him? The cows do not know them, the contented cows with their lip prints each one different.

'Keep breathing, Sara, just keep breathing,' Frank liked to say.

I carefully step over the place where they had been standing at the graveside, carefully so as not to damage Frank's signature in the brown mud. His name remembered to himself as if a hero in the fields of France. FRANK. The letters etched deeply into the stamped-down dust, neat and all in a straight row, as if there is no such thing as a rainstorm, nothing to wash them away.

Frank continues his speech as we walk.

'They are advertising for miners up there, Shabane Asbestos, I could start September first if nothing better comes up. Still, up north, land of opportunity it is, you don't get the Afrikaner up there, not so much. Wonderful, man. Sara, are you interested in coming with us?'

Then and again and again, still years later with no warning, I feel Herbert suddenly thrown into the room like a bat of the night. He cracks into the soft sky as if a teacup breaking. Don't know what it is so hard he comes up against when all the world seems soft.

Ahead of us Sybil heaves her large frame over the rough clumps of grasses alongside Frank. I do not understand why she does not walk behind him on the path, but that is Sybil for you, not one to come in second place, despite her quiet nature. I look beyond to Cora's gait far out in front of us, leading the way. She can maintain a surprising pace despite that odd little step like a bird. We catch up properly with Frank and Sybil just as they reach the cemetery offices.

'So, Sara, what do you think? You coming north?' Frank motions towards his hearse. 'Plenty of space. Lovely. Come on.'

I look across at Hafferjee and shake my head. You will not see me, Sara Highbury, getting into a hearse before my time.

We stand at the gates. Frank pulls away and walks over to the hearse. Cranes his neck inches from the tyres' treads, examines them one by one for defects. There are no flies on Frank, not yet. He takes care what he purchases. The autumn rains begin to fall. The first drops stick the shirt's thin white fabric to Frank's back as the imprint of scattered coins. That kind of rain always comes from low-lying clouds, that's how the drops can be so big. Or so I told Maggie once. I wonder now if she still recalls it, there where she is, not so far away now, soon I will see her. I gulp a breath of Frank as we say farewell.

His skin still has the smell of machinery grease from those large syrup tins that he used to scoop greeny-yellow by the handful to lather over a joint, all fermented in with garlic and brandy – just like I knew him on the mines. He is his own unique blend that I drink, punch-drunk yet sober as a church mouse.

I hear the singing and wailing long before they come into view. Some fifty souls marching, coming over the rise, on their way to the native cemetery beyond, further down the road. Louder and louder until the earth itself is humming along. A procession all dressed in white. The person in front shakes a tambourine, feet shuffle a forward-back step in the dust, forward and back, but still they move as one. Cora tries to ape them as they come past, bending low at the knees and standing heavy on the back of her high-heeled shoes, swaying side to side. I stand quietly in the rain, feeling no discomfort from it. But that rhythm I do not know. I have never been much of a one for dancing. And that is when I look across at Hafferjee and I tell him that he must come with me to find Maggie, for I wish to bring her home. The closest I came to dancing were the nights I spent with him.

One day later and I am standing here on the threshold of the Hafferjee house. The same house where once, almost twenty years before, I had delivered a note addressed to Mr A. Hafferjee, and stood there, looking at the split colour of the Impatiens lining the floor. I have never in all these years been inside – despite my impatience. Impatience, that is a condition that he has been full of all of his life. Time is always running out.

A young man answers the door. He seems to be expecting me. Perhaps he is one of those from the photograph Hafferjee showed me so long ago, I forget their names and so I cannot ask. The boy tells me to follow him inside. Indoors, the house is packed about with things. Strange smells that I cannot define, sweet and sour and steamy. Through a door from the passage I glimpse a woman standing draped in a purple sari that does not cover her thick bare ankles. Her fleshy feet speckled with white flour are visible beneath a wooden table. Is this Hafferjee's wife? As I move on through to the next room, I see her strong hands, their veins showing blue beneath her dry honey skin, slap back and forth, a flat chapatti bread dough helpless between them. Perhaps it is a mealtime, there are so many pots of hot food about, their lids tightly covering though steam escaping here and there. I do not feel hungry. I walk across the red and blue pattern of the carpet, beneath the ornate chandeliers heavy in the ceiling, follow the rich embroidery of the boy's waistcoat. Finally he shows me in to a sort of sitting room, odd chairs and a table strewn about, two chairs stacked in a corner for no reason of seating that I can imagine. I wait here, and then Amin joins me. Now and then a woman or older sort of child appears in the room, and disappears just as silently; they do not meet my eye in greeting. Amin ignores some of these strangers as if they do not exist, others, he sends out. In the midst of these comings and goings, without introduction or embellishment, he begins to speak. Yes, it is his turn to speak here in his own house. He speaks quickly, in the rapid way that an Indian has. What he says shows me well enough that Amin has now told his family here everything about me and about Anna and Maggie too. There are no secrets any longer, about our short spell of love so long ago, the carnation that indeed had brought bad luck as I had feared, and his visit to me at the boarding house for guidance regarding his responsibilities now that he knew he had fathered a child outside of wedlock.

I walk over to take a closer look at the pictures on the mantel. Amin is there, littered all about with other photographs, preserved for all time in a gilt-edged frame. None here in this gallery that I know and none know me. I look at the man before me through the haze of oily cooking smells becoming now more pronounced, their strength stinging my eyes. Look, and can only pray that I will not be offered any food in this house, for my stomach is churning and unable to eat, and I believe it would be a rudeness to refuse. That these people, so sure in their unknown ways, will think me a common woman, not knowing how things are done proper. As if he can read my thoughts, Amin shakes his bent dark head, the dense hair fitting his head like a cap, it gleams with oil, alive the way it used to be, so that I have to look away in shame. I tell Hafferjee that I have telephoned the nuns and they have given a date when it would be convenient to come to discuss Maggie's future. We agree that when we fetch Maggie to bring her home we will tell her all about her mother, everything we know, and that she will hear from Hafferjee his own stories.

When I had taken Maggie's mother, Anna, on at the sweatshop, what interested me were her nimble fingers, her sharp mind and her will to obey. And I gave her comfort, made her a quilt even, and not from scraps either, but from my own favourite cloth. Then one by one she had shed the things I knew of her, as skin after skin left apart from her. Much like a snake does, she moved on. There is no sin in that, I intend to tell Maggie the same. One day Anna had stood on the top step at Pauline Kraemer's house in the Cape, her back to me, she stooped to pick up her bags. The girl slithered away, slipped through life free of man and beast.

'I am going to my uncle in Magiesfontein,' she had said.

She looked so resolute and, yes, hard, a hardness already visible, that I did not ask Anna how long she intended to be gone.

A woman comes in whilst Amin and I are still speaking. She wipes the glass over a gilt-framed photograph of Hafferjee, his face beside his wife in younger years that is standing there on the mantelpiece. She separates the picture from the other trinkets, wraps it in a sort of soft white cloth and packs it away into some sort of cupboard that I had not noticed. Having done this to her satisfaction, the woman takes a last look across at Hafferjee and then she walks out. I can't help wondering how many other family members are stuffed away in that cupboard.

The woman seemed too young to be Hafferjee's wife, and the shape of her face not at all like the photograph. I think of the picture he pulled from his breast that night so many years ago. Who but a wife would take a florist pin and with such a steady hand bring it so close to a man's heart?

Sitting in the Hafferjee house now, with Amin before me, sweet smells issuing from his kitchen, Amin's pictures no longer on the mantel, a spider motionless against the white ceiling, two of his legs bent over a ridge where the ceiling is embossed with a line marking out a new pattern, sitting there, I see it is time now to go. And I know that Hafferjee will grow steadily more distant, as if a passing ship's inexorable path across the ocean out, far out to the horizon.

We walk and all the way our arms are linked, uncaring who may see us. As we approach the boarding house, Hafferjee releases his arm in order to take my key and unlock the door. His embrace has a new awkwardness to it. Still, it is open as I always knew it. You will seldom find such an embrace from a white man – theirs are more like gardens with barbed wire around them, compared to this that has no fences. It is an awkward farewell beside the seedlings that I have planted here at the boarding house, to remind me of him.

As I go about my tasks for the evening, checking on the residents, and ensuring the kitchen is equipped for the menus for the week, I wonder to myself whether Hafferjee's wife, like I had, brushes with the lengths of her finger his short black hair bristling in the moonlight. A wife would not celebrate how Hafferjee, sweet in his hesitation and resoluteness, had once entered my workroom like a boy. Does she, like I once did, carefully circle the shiny patch of scalp in its small beginnings at the crown of Hafferjee's head? That little patch of baldness, so tender and spongy that one can almost feel the muffled brain underneath pumping out its thoughts.

Tomorrow we will fetch Maggie from the home in which they have put her, we will fetch her and tell her everything she wants to know.

8

I know that Floss is shuffling down the corridor. I can
hear the master key clanging against her other keys as it
dangles from the blue string around her neck. She can go
anywhere with that key. I know that she has been into
my room when I am not there. I have returned more than
once to careless signs left by her ferreting – my dresser
drawer left ajar, a pink tissue dropped from a pocket. It
is as if there is something in her that wants to be found
out. I think of the possibility of Floss coming into the room
now, shuffling across the carpet, its flower petals shaped
like peacock feathers, yet all the wrong colours, in reds
and oranges and mustard yellow. I imagine Floss walking
in and seeing Maggie asleep here in my bed. For I am not
allowed to keep a lodger, not even a family member, here
in the boarding house. The room is for my use alone. No
matter. I look across at the half moon of Maggie's finger-
nails against the coverlet as she sleeps.

We fetched her only yesterday. It is therefore not
surprising that I do not know what the future holds.
Hafferjee had come with me, as I said that he should.
We took the 5.30 a.m. train from Cape Town and around
midday disembarked at Langlaagte station.

We found the home without much difficulty. The nuns pointed Maggie out in the garden, as if I did not know her. She stood with her bad posture, half facing a rose bush full in bloom. She had been so thin when she lived with me, all arms and legs. I was shocked to see the pounds that she had gained – they have rounded her face and made even her small hands puffy. When she saw me she came forward, as if some sort of a giant expecting an embrace. I had to remind myself over and over that she is just a child, not yet twelve. And where was Hafferjee? Walked off down the road? Hiding behind a tree? Strange how this weight and bearing begin to come to some girls this age, but not all. These young girls for no fault of their own are suddenly ashamed and soft and silent. Is it because of their sudden size, inhabiting bodies much larger and clumsier than themselves? I had an urge to straighten her up, hold her, make her proud, if only that were within my power.

We sat together for a while on an empty bench in the garden of the home. Her hair surprised me, it was as if stuck in waves about her face. Her face, once so alert with questions, was a little greyish-yellow, like a caracal. A sprinkling of small pimples, like Frank's asbestos fibre rash, had spread across the surface of her nose. And what she said next shattered my heart into a thousand splinters.

'I don't mind staying here, if you don't want me,' she said. And her voice was so soft and stuttering that I had to twist to the side to watch her lips as they moved. As she spoke, Maggie looked away, up at the iron roof of the shelter, out at the fields beyond.

'Look at me when you talk, child; have you forgotten your manners? If there is one thing I cannot abide, it is a child who talks to the rooftops and expects a person to answer.'

Maggie startled. Wounds deeper than the scar tissue still slung across her arm. We spoke a little more then without fuss and she agreed to come home with me. She reached for my arm, and suggested that we go indoors.

The lady at the desk looked up and motioned us through.

'Number thirty-two,' she said.

So I accompanied Maggie to her room and I packed her bags, whilst she sat cross-legged on the floor. There was another bed there. I still do not know the name of the child who slept beside Maggie night after night there in the home. She has not yet spoken of it. Whilst I folded her blanket, Maggie sat on the wooden floor watching, only now and then reminding me about her toothbrush, or hairbrush, or the stamp album still sitting in the box beneath her bed. A small patch of afternoon sunlight fell onto her face through the window. She rocked her body to and fro, in and out of the shadow. The motion of a creature who does not even know she is moving, her body seemed taken over from without, the motion of a young mother rocking a small child in her arms. Perhaps I would wrap her blanket around her, lift her onto the bed to sleep.

Hafferjee was still pacing up and down in the garden.

'Be careful of the night terrors,' the staff told me before we left.

On the way back to Cape Town, an old man came into the compartment in which we were seated. The trains have changed now and I have too, for with Hafferjee I cannot travel in the white carriage, so we sit together in the non-whites, a holy trinity that none dare contest, Hafferjee, Maggie and me. The carriage would have been empty were it not for the three of us and this old coloured man just stepped in whose eyes shook in his head with the motion of the train like a porcelain doll. He seemed to be waiting for something. Not for decay, but for news. Any sort. I looked across at Maggie and felt the inevitability of the train on its tracks, the relentless path forward. A train of fourteen carriages takes 3.5 minutes to come to a standstill from a speed of four miles per hour. This is the kind of information poster up in the station master's office, a safety warning of sorts. If a man dived as if from a board, into the tracks, as if into the sea, right into the path of the train, as if to catch an ocean's breaker, in a millisecond he would be gone. A severed head would be flung against the embankment and roll a little way before coming to a standstill beside a waterlogged wild dagga bush, setting its yellow flowers waving in the breeze.

They say time heals, but that has not been my experience. No, everything that ever happens to a person is forever written in the body's cells, that is what I see.

Here in the boarding house, Floss shuffles by outside my room with her key. Her feet barely lift from the floor. I can picture her face, a dull mask of itself. I can't help myself wondering how she looked when she was this age that Maggie is now, almost twelve. Further on down the corridor I hear Cora's high-pitched laughter – Mr Silverstein seems to have become quite the comedian here since Cora met him. None of this wakes Maggie, still exhausted from her journey, still growing in her sleep.

Acknowledgements

I would like to thank my grandfather Frederick Frances Wakefield, for the years of correspondence and conversation that enriched *The Shape of Him* immeasurably. Thanks too to Jane Fox and the late Lionel Abrahams of Johannesburg for their generosity and enthusiasm regarding everything to do with the early drafts of this book. And to Theunis, Hannah and Sarah Roux for everything else that matters.

www.vintage-books.co.uk